# These Seven

*have you read*

# These Seven

*Nottingham writers?*

*John Harvey*
*Megan Taylor*
*Brick*
*Paula Rawsthorne*
*Alison Moore*
*Shreya Sen Handley*
*Alan Sillitoe*

*Five Leaves Bookshop*

# These Seven

Published in 2015 by Five Leaves Bookshop in association with Bromley House Library and Nottingham Writers' Studio in support of the Nottingham City of Literature project Nottingham's Stories

www.fiveleavesbookshop.co.uk

Edited by Ross Bradshaw

*ISBN 978-1-910170-20-5*

Supported using public funding by

**ARTS COUNCIL
ENGLAND**

LOTTERY FUNDED

Nottingham's Stories is supported
by Arts Council England
through Grants for the Arts

Cover design:
Pippa Hennessy/Five Leaves Bookshop

Typeset and design:
Four Sheets Design and Print

Printed by
Russell Press in Nottingham

# Contents

# Introduction

This book came out of a conversation that started with 'What about...?' and sped through 'Maybe we could...' to 'OK, let's do it!' alarmingly quickly. It wouldn't have got much further than that if it hadn't been for the enthusiastic response of the writers we approached and then the encouragement of our partners in the UNESCO City of Literature bid which gave us the confidence to approach the Arts Council for funding.

It wasn't long before the book had become part of a whole new project, Nottingham's Stories, an initiative that could involve anyone living in and around Nottingham even if they didn't normally seek out opportunities for reading and writing and talking about our city. We love these stories and think they are just right to share with people of all ages and backgrounds.

We will be sending them and their writers out into schools and community groups, libraries and public places, the parts of our city excitement about reading doesn't always reach. In our writing workshops we will be encouraging you to develop and share your stories. Who knows? We might discover some of Nottingham's future writing stars.

So here they are. Seven stories to read and talk about and be inspired by. We hope you enjoy them and go on to read some of the other terrific Nottingham writers we didn't have space to include.

Our special thanks go to Ruth Fainlight who has given us permission to include one of her late husband Alan Sillitoe's stories, to the novelist Nicola Monaghan who will be reading and talking about his work and running some of our workshops, to the Arts Council and to all the organisations and groups who have agreed to host our readings and workshops.

*Sheelagh Gallagher*
Bromley House

*Ross Bradshaw*
Five Leaves

*Pippa Hennessy*
Nottingham Writers' Studio

# Ask Me Now

*John Harvey*

Tom Whitemore's father left him a set of golf clubs he had yet to use, a collection of the maritime novels of Patrick O'Brian, and an abiding love of Louis Armstrong and Duke Ellington.

Few visits to the retirement chalet in Devon where the older man lived out his last days were allowed to pass without his father reminiscing about the time he had seen Louis on a revolving stage at the Empress Hall, his warm-up act a one-legged tap dancer called Peg Leg Bates; or the Ellington concert when the young English tenor player, Tubby Hayes, had walked on stage, mid-number, and, to the audience's amazed recognition, taken the vacant seat in an otherwise all-American all-star saxophone section.

No matter how many times told, Whitemore listened to the stories with pleasure, sharing, for a few vicarious moments, his father's delight at the former, the surge of patriotism as he relived the latter. Try as he might, he could never quite bring himself to believe in the one-legged dancer.

Louis, though... when his father had suffered his third and fatal heart attack, Armstrong's trumpet had been

9

pealing out a succession of high Cs in the final chorus of 'Hotter Than That', each one clear as a bell; the album still slowly revolving on the turntable when the carer had found his father's body wedged between his wheelchair and a chest of drawers, the stylus trapped in the run-off groove, fast against the label.

In contrast, all Whitemore's wife had left him, the day she drove off to her parents in Chapel St. Leonard's, taking the twins, was a note propped against the burned-out toaster in the kitchen.

*I'm sorry, Tom, I can't take it any more. I just can't...*

That had been six years ago.

His father had been dead for ten.

Whitemore was still in the same house, a lodger upstairs in the twins' room Monday to Friday, and he was still doing the same job — the one his wife had hated — detective sergeant in the Public Protection Team: domestic violence, hate crime, serious sexual abuse, assault.

*Scum, Tom, that's what they are. Who you spend your days and nights with. Scum of the earth and then you bring them home to us.*

She turned aside from his face, flinched at his touch. Flinched when he held one or other of the twins in his arms, helped them to undress, softly kissed the tops of their heads, ran the flannel across them in the bath.

*I'm sorry, Tom...*

For a while, the first year or so, if not more, he had allowed himself to think it was temporary, a break to clear the air; sooner or later things would even out, Marianne would come to her senses, move back home with the children. His children. She couldn't stay with her parents for ever, after all.

So Whitemore drove out to see them every other weekend without fail: spent time with the boys, a game of soccer on the beach then late Sunday lunch around the table, Yorkshire pudding, roast potatoes, gravy. Barely a voice raised over whatever music was playing, subdued, in the next room. The twins keeping their eyes on their plates, snatching an occasional glance at dad or mum.

"Boys," Marianne's mother said abruptly one afternoon, when he was in the kitchen, helping with the washing up. "Young boys especially. More than anything they need a father." Smiling faintly, she handed him a dry tea towel. "That's what I think, at least. Not that anyone's asked."

Encouraged, Whitemore smiled back.

He hadn't quite understood.

Marianne followed him out to the car and suggested they take a walk before he left. It was coming on dark, the wind relenting off the sea. Faint in the distance, the lights of Skegness.

*Tom, I've met someone...*

Bile rose high in his throat and stuck.

All he remembered of the divorce was signing papers, feeling numb. They were going to live in Lincoln, Marianne and the children, the new husband, close by the cathedral, a new home, ready and waiting. When he got to see the twins now it was more awkward, less often: listless afternoons in Burger King straining for something to say. Biting his tongue while the boys flicked ketchup-coated fries at one another when they thought he wasn't looking, kicking each other beneath the table, harder and harder until he finally snapped.

He'd not long returned from one such visit, the afternoon ending in sour looks and recrimination, when the phone shook him out of his misery. Heather Jeffries, the senior social worker attached to the team, low-voiced, level-headed.

"Tom, hoped I might catch you. The meeting in the morning — any chance of a coffee beforehand?"

There was a café off the Old Market Square — in truth, there were several, this one quieter, less fashionable.

11

Formica tables. Posters of old Italian movies on the wall. Whitemore thought he recognised Gina Lollobrigida, Sophia Loren.

The choice of coffees was simple: large or small, white or black. He placed his order, picked up the cups from the counter and carried them across.

Heather dropped two tiny sweeteners into hers and stirred. "Emma Laurie, Tom, ring any bells...?"

Whitemore pictured a wraith-like woman with wispy hair, cigarette burns on her arms. Late twenties, looking older. For a time she'd lived with a man he'd been supervising, an ex-offender: it had not gone well.

"Three kids, wasn't it?" Whitemore said. "All taken into care. Rory, Jason and... I don't remember the girl... Julie, maybe?"

"Jade. The boys are both fostered out now — together by some small miracle and happy as Larry. Jade's been back home with her mum the best part of a year. A few wobbles, but until recently it's seemed to be just about okay."

"And now?"

"Helen Bailey, she's the family's social worker..."

"I know Helen."

"Three times she's been round in the last few weeks wanting to see Jade and each time there's been some excuse. Sorry, but Jade's on a sleepover with a friend; Jade's been up all night with a poorly tummy, throwing up and everything, and now she's upstairs sleeping — could Helen not come back another time rather than wake her? When she went back the next day as arranged, there was nobody there. Phoned that evening to see what had happened; bloke Emma's been seeing had borrowed his mate's van and taken them off to Mablethorpe for the day. Surprise treat."

"And Helen, she thinks there's more to it?"

"Wouldn't you?"

12

"Likely."

"Last thing she wants, Helen, a situation where she keeps getting fobbed off till it's too late. For the girl's sake as well as her own. Jade ends up in hospital or worse and it's Helen's name that's splashed all over the paper. Another social worker falling down on the job. The media only too anxious to hang her out to dry. Neglect and worse. People baying for her blood."

"You really think it's that serious? For Jade, I mean."

"That's it, I just don't know. Helen could be being over-cautious, reading the signs wrongly..." Jeffries sighed, pushed her cup aside. "There's another thing. Emma's pregnant again. Three months since. I thought she might opt for a termination, but no. Left to herself, maybe she would have, and maybe for the best. But this man, the new boyfriend..."

"He's the father?"

Jeffries nodded. "Wheelan. Garry Wheelan. Two Rs. Won't hear of it. Like it was his decision, not hers."

"And what? Another child, a baby, you're afraid she won't cope?"

"I don't think she'll find it easy. If there is something going on with Jade, especially."

"And this Wheelan...?"

"Ex-army. Local."

"Anything known? Cause for concern?"

"Ran the DBS checks, naturally. Three arrests in as many years. Two for common assault, one for criminal damage. Never charged."

"This was before he got together with Emma or after?"

"Before."

"And he was in the army how long?"

"Ten years, give or take."

"Afghanistan?"

"Yes. Iraq before that."

Whitemore looked to where the inside of the window was

13

beaded with condensation. "It takes time to settle back into normal life, you know that as well as anyone. Perhaps this was what he needed. Chance to settle down."

"I'd like to think so."

"But you don't."

"I'm worried, Tom, that's all. Emma and Jade, it's been touch and go like I say. Come close once or twice to Jade going back into care. And Emma, as we know, she's not been brilliant at coping. Add a baby, an ex-squaddie with a temper; a proclivity, maybe, for violence. All together in that little two up, two down."

"This will all come up at the meeting."

"I know, but..."

"But you thought I might ask around, circumstances of those arrests. Put a little flesh on the bones. Have a word with him later, perhaps? If it seems appropriate. Garry with two Rs."

Heather smiled. "You'll keep Helen in the loop?"

"Of course."

She glanced at her watch. "Best get our skates on. Don't want them starting without us."

Two days later, when Whitemore finally made it home after a more-than-twelve-hour shift, head throbbing and only a week-old ready meal from Sainsbury's between himself and what felt like near starvation, the missed call light on his phone was glowing.

"Tom, hi. It's Helen. I tried your mobile earlier. Give me a call if you get a chance, okay?"

He listened to the message again before pressing erase; fished a packet of ibuprofen from the kitchen drawer, set the kettle to boil and dropped a tea bag into the Forest mug one of the twins, Adam, had bought him for Christmas. Ignoring the date on the Thai chicken curry, he placed it in the microwave and flicked the switch.

A considerable part of his morning had been spent with a seventeen-year-old rape victim, who had decided, after

14

being harassed on Twitter, Facebook and Instagram, to withdraw the complaint against her attacker. After which, together with a member of the probation service and a social worker, he'd sat round a table at the Hockley office of Recovery in Nottingham, determining which of the available programmes would be most suitable for a twenty-two-year-old who'd gone into prison clean and been released with a serious drug problem eighteen months later.

He tipped the food out on to a plate and unfolded that day's copy of the *Post*. Plans to extend the city's tram network were set to go ahead. A mass brawl outside a takeaway in Aspley had resulted in three men being taken to Queen's Medical Centre with serious injuries. After picking at the curry a while longer he forked the remainder into the bin.

"Helen? Hi, it's Tom. Just got your message."

Sometimes callers on the landline seemed oddly distant, their voices blurred across several time lines; Helen Bailey's was so clear she could have been in the next room.

"Garry Wheelan, you haven't had a chance...?"

"No, I'm sorry."

"No problem. I know you're busy. It's just I went round there, Emma's, this afternoon. Caught a glimpse of Jade in the other room before they could scoot her away. Plaster to one side of her head, what looked like bruising. She fell, Garry said when I asked..."

"Garry said...?"

"Yes. Racing round the back ginnel like a silly thing, he said, went sprawling. I asked did they take her to A & E in case, you know, there was a concussion, but no, he said, why all that fuss? Emma washed it clean, stuck on a plaster and kissed it better."

"And Jade?"

"She seemed all right, I suppose. Not easy to tell."

"Kids fall over," Whitemore said. "It's what they do. Happens all the time."

It hung in the air between them, buoyed up by the faint sound of her breathing.

"I'll get on to it," Whitemore said. "First thing."

He was halfway through dialling his ex-wife's number, over a week since he'd spoken to the twins, when he reconsidered — if they hadn't turned in already there would be some barbed remark from Marianne about getting them all excited just before bedtime.

Twenty minutes of the news and he was ready for bed himself, knowing that once there he'd find it hard to fall asleep. How wrong could he be? Next he knew it was 4.30 in the morning and he needed to pee.

\*\*\*

The street was short and narrow, the houses squat and, here and there, in sore need of care. Emma Laurie's lay towards the far end, where the terrace halted abruptly at a patch of barren ground. Mismatching curtains were closed across the windows, shutting out the meagre light.

Stepping up to the door, Whitemore's mind was hauled back sharply seven years: the death of Emma's previous partner at his own hand, a Stanley knife resting on the bath edge alongside a pale oval of soap. In a ramshackle shed in the back yard, children's faces staring up at him from the cloistered dark.

"You! What the fuck you doin' here?"

"Hello, Emma."

Hair pulled harshly back from her face, tiredness darkening her eyes, she was wearing grey sweat pants and a matching hoodie, the baby just starting to show.

"I was close by," Whitemore said. "Thought I'd stop off and see how you were."

"Lyin' bastard." Said with the hint of a smile.

He followed her inside, through a room where clothes hung drying before one bar of an electric fire and into a

16

kitchen with a folding table pushed to one side, plates and bowls in the sink waiting to be washed; the faint smell of toast.

Emma rinsed out a couple of mugs, took a carton of milk from the fridge. There was an ultrasound image fixed to the fridge door.

"How's it going?" Whitemore asked. "The baby?"

She shrugged.

"Boy or girl?"

"Not gonna matter, is it?"

"How d'you mean?"

"Your lot, soon as I've dropped it, fallin' over backwards for the chance to take it away."

"Come on, Emma, that's not true."

"No? Why's that skinny bitch round here all the time then, sticking her nose in?"

"Helen, you mean?"

"Always questions. Questions, questions, questions. Jade, how's she eatin', is she putting on weight, how's she gettin' on at school? Like it was her business. How'd she get that bruise? Cut the size of my little fingernail and it's did we take her to doctor, take her up to A & E..."

"She's concerned."

"Concerned, all right. Bending her scrawny arse over backwards, lookin' for a reason to hoik Jade back into care. Baby too, when it comes."

"Emma, I don't think it's like that at all."

"No? Well, you would say that, wouldn't you? Sugar in this or not?"

Emma moved the washing away from the fire and switched on the extra bar. They sat either side of the flat screen TV, framed photos of Jade and her two brothers on the narrow ledge above the fireplace; Jade smiling uncertainly towards the camera, a stray length of hair falling across her face; both lads secondary school age by now, straight and proud in their uniforms — what had

17

Heather Jeffries said? Happy as Larry? — new family, new lives. They would be, Whitemore thought, around the same age as his own.

"Do you see much of them?" he asked. "The boys?"

"Christmas. Birthdays. Might bump into 'em once in a while, you know, round town." She shook her head. "Garry wanted to take 'em to City Ground one time. You'd've thought he wanted to cart 'em off other side of the bloody world."

"I was hoping Garry might be around."

"How's that, then?"

"Just a chat."

"Not in any trouble, is he?"

"Not as far as I know."

"Sorted himself out has Garry. Since he's been with me. Quietened down."

"That's good to hear."

"Still gets these headaches, mind. Trouble sleeping. But he's quit the drinking. Bar a pint or two, weekends." She lit a cigarette from the fire. "Quiet, too. Too much so for my liking, sometimes. Sits where you are, staring off into space, God knows where he really is, but wherever it is it's not here. Back there somewhere, I suppose. Some godforsaken place or other."

Whitemore nodded, sipped his tea. The sound of someone's television was leaking through from next door; the bass beat of a car stereo parked close by.

"You don't know when he might be back?"

Emma shook her head. "Once he's out, he's out all day. Till Jade gets home at least. You could try the library, Angel Row. Sits in there sometimes and reads. Or the Arboretum. Wanders round there, the rose garden, says it clears his head."

There was no sign of Garry Wheelan in the library. By the time Whitemore reached the Arboretum, cutting

18

down past the southern edge of the cemetery, a faint rain had begun to fall. Wheelan was sitting on one of the benches surrounding the Chinese Bell pagoda, close by the cannons brought back in triumph from the Crimean War. Green waterproof jacket, boots, jeans; lean face, pale eyes, dark hair clipped short.

He scarcely looked up as Whitemore approached.

Said nothing as he sat down.

"I'm..." Whitemore began.

"I know who you are. Emma texted me, said you'd likely be nosing round."

"I just wanted..."

"To have a chat, she said. Didn't say what about."

"Cases like Emma's..."

"That what she is? A case?"

"Situations like Emma's, where there's been some concern in the past about the children in her care. We have to think about the appropriateness of any close relationships she may have formed..."

"That nonce, Darren?"

"Yes, Darren..."

"Pathetic bastard."

"Maybe." The bathroom door had been bolted from the inside; one of his arms had hung down inside the bath, the other trailed towards the floor.

"You're not saying I'm like him? That prick. 'Cause if you are..." Wheelan facing him now, one of his boots starting to beat a slow tattoo on the ground.

Whitemore held his gaze, waiting for him to relax.

"That bother you got yourself into a while back, I've been talking to the officers concerned. From what I can tell, it was mostly a case of you getting drawn into something not of your making. The last time, for instance..."

"Ignorant bastard, mouthing off about the army. Got what he was asking for."

"Got you into trouble."

"It was worth it."

"You think so?"

Wheelan shook his head. "It's different now."

Close to where they were sitting a blackbird was busily arguing a worm from the soil.

"You want to walk for a bit?" Whitemore said.

They went up past the pagoda towards the Addison Street entrance and turned right along the road that would take them down by the university buildings and into the city centre.

"Emma mentioned you'd been having trouble sleeping."

No reply. The rain a little heavier now. Wheelan staring straight ahead.

"Bad dreams, maybe? Headaches that won't go away?"

"Know it all, don't you?"

"Bits and pieces. Men I've had some contact with in the past. Odd things I've read."

Wheelan laughed derisively. "Things you've fucking read!"

They came to halt at the junction with Shakespeare Street, the Orange Tree pub in front of them, the old library at their backs.

"You know there's help available, people you can speak to..."

"Yeah. Sit round and — what was it? — explore your emotions and trauma in the company of fellow sufferers. Well, bollocks to that. What I want to do is shut that crap out of my mind once and for all, not bring it all back so's some psychiatrist can wet himself. Write a fucking book about it."

He was several strides away when Whitemore called him back.

"Being a father to Emma's baby. Being responsible. How d'you feel about that?"

"You got kids?"

"Yes. Two."

"Then how d'you think I feel? Ask your fucking self."

The next day began with Whitemore doing his best to reassure the mother of a vulnerable sixteen-year-old in custody that every effort would be made to ensure he did no further self-harm, and ended with a lengthy meeting at which Ben Leonard, the community psychiatric nurse attached to the unit, introduced a new set of proposals for safely re-integrating offenders with mental health issues back into the community.

It was past eight and dark by the time he got home; the rain that had started earlier that day still falling. There was a heavy-looking bundle on the path beside the front door.

As Whitemore drew closer the bundle moved and raised its head. It was his son, Adam.

Whitemore eased him inside, stripped off his sodden coat, towelled his hair, chafed warmth back into his hands. Careful, so far, to avoid asking what he was doing there, all the other questions busy in his mind.

Fifteen or so minutes later, Adam dwarfed inside one of his father's jumpers, central heating turned up to full, they were sitting across from one another, mugs of hot chocolate in their hands.

Looking at him, trying not to stare at the tousled hair, the almost-violet skin around the boy's downturned eyes, Whitemore felt something lurch inside him. Love, for want of a better name.

"Do they know you're here?"

"Who?"

"Mum and... and Colin."

"Course not."

"I'll have to phone them."

"No."

"Adam, I must. They'll be worried sick."

21

"Not now. Not yet."

"I have to."

There were three missed calls on his mobile; texts he hadn't read; after switching his phone off for the meeting he'd forgotten to switch it back on.

Marianne picked up at the first ring.

"Adam, is he...?"

"He's here."

"Thank God."

Behind Marianne's relieved sobs, Whitemore could hear a man's voice, urgent and questioning.

"I'd only just got back," Whitemore said, "and he was here waiting."

"How on earth did he get all that way?"

"By train."

"But how...?"

"Money he got for Christmas, that's what he said."

"And he's all right?"

"He's fine."

The same voice again in the background — Colin's, he assumed — raised in exasperation. "All right, all right," he heard Marianne saying. "But just wait, please."

"Fine!" and a door slamming.

The click of a glass and then the sound of his wife — his ex-wife — lighting a cigarette, exhaling.

"He told his brother," Marianne said, "he was going to a friend's house to play some game or other. Colin went round to collect him. That was the first we knew."

"He says Colin hit him."

"What?"

"Adam. He says Colin hit him. That's why he ran away."

"It was nothing."

"Really?"

"Just some silly argument over nothing at all."

"His phone. That's what it was about. That's what he says."

"He wouldn't stop fiddling with it, all through dinner. No matter how many times he was told not to."

"And when he didn't stop Colin hit him."

"No."

"He didn't hit him, is that what you're saying?"

"Not because of that."

"Then why?"

"Colin took the phone away from him, tried to, and Adam told him to fuck off."

"And that's when he hit him?"

"He lost his temper. It happens."

"How often?"

"Sorry?"

"How often does he lose his temper?"

"He doesn't."

"No? Adam says he slapped him round the back of the head so hard it knocked him out of his chair. Or is that an exaggeration?"

"No." Quietly. "No, it's not."

There were things Whitemore wanted to say best left to another day.

"I'll drive him back over in the morning."

"Thank you."

Whitemore broke the connection.

The sky had cleared into a conglomeration of muted blues and greys, the spire of the cathedral rising into view when they were still some way distant. Whitemore had pressed play on the car stereo as they were approaching Newark, shuffled through Ellington at Newport, Basie, Louis Armstrong at the Crescendo, but none had suited his mood.

Adam had barely spoken for most of the journey, sitting hunched in the passenger seat, barely moving save occasionally to shift his balance, check his phone. At breakfast he had asked, not looking up as he did so, why did he have to stay living in Lincoln, why couldn't he move back to Nottingham, live there with him?

"It's not that straightforward," Whitemore said.

"Why not? I'm here, aren't I?" Adam looking at him now. "You don't have to take me back at all. Not today. They can just send my clothes, right? Anything else I need. And I'll get to change schools. Somewhere where I won't be being picked on all the time."

"Is that what happens?"

Adam pushed his bowl away. "Why can't I do that? Why? Go on, just tell me why."

"Look, Adam, you're only saying all this because you're still angry and upset."

"I'm not."

"I think you are. And besides, imagine what it'd be like. You'd scarcely know anyone for one thing, wouldn't have any friends..."

"I could make new friends."

"You'd miss Matthew... and your mum."

"Yeah, well, least I wouldn't be living with him. Bloody Colin."

Whitemore sighed, looked at his watch. "We ought to be making a move."

On the way out to the car Adam caught hold of his sleeve. "Dad. Seriously. Why can't I? Move back here, I mean."

"It wasn't what we agreed."

"Who? Who agreed? Not me."

"Me and your mum."

"That's not fair."

"I know."

Whitemore reached out to touch his son's hair, but the boy swerved smartly away.

As soon as the front door opened, Adam scuttled in under his mother's gaze and scurried upstairs, leaving Whitemore not knowing whether to kiss Marianne briefly on the cheek or stand there smiling half-heartedly and wait.

"Well," she said, "you'd better come in."

The kitchen was at the back of the house, looking out over the garden; an extension, partly covered in glass.

"Coffee, Tom?"

"No, it's okay."

"It's no problem."

"All right, then. Thanks."

When he saw her now, it was impossible to understand what there had ever been between them.

"How is he?" Marianne asked. "Adam?"

"Hurt. Angry. He says he wants to move out, come and live with me."

"Of course he does."

"Why of course?"

"He was too young to remember what it was like."

Whitemore gazed out into the garden: neat clumps of shrubs, compost, a football, in one corner a camellia coming into bloom.

"Colin's not here then?"

"No. He had to go to work. A meeting..."

"Some client with wealth management problems, I don't doubt."

"Tom, don't start..."

"Bespoke financial plan in need a bit of buffering."

"Christ, Tom!"

"What?"

"You know how... how petty you sound? How bloody self-righteous?"

"Well, whatever he's doing, he's not here is he, that's the point. And he's not here because he hasn't got the guts, after what he's done, to see me face to face."

"What were you going to do, then, Tom? Punch him one? Arrest him?"

"Maybe both."

"God, you really are pathetic."

"Yes, well, we know that, don't we? And what you were ever doing, wasting five years of your precious life with me, we'll never fucking know!"

Marianne pulled both hands deliberately away from the tray she was carrying, letting coffee pot, jug, cups and saucers crash to the floor.

"Stop it!" Adam screamed from the doorway, face distorting. "Stop it, why don't you? Just stop!"

\*\*\*

A change in the weather, is that really all it took? Mornings when the air was crisp, the light clear and more shades of blue in the sky than you could ever hope to identify.

Whitemore dug out an old pair of trainers from the bottom of the wardrobe and started going for a morning run. Marianne, relenting, trying to rebuild bridges, said if he had any leave owing, why didn't he take the twins away for a few days during their Easter break? Whitemore booked them into a B & B in Whitby, up on the North Yorks coast, visited the abbey, played football on the beach, tramped across the cliffs to Robin Hood's Bay and sat high above the tide line eating fish and chips.

Enjoying an after work drink with Helen Bailey one evening, she told him any worries she'd had about Jade were almost certainly unfounded; Emma's pregnancy was progressing pretty much as normal, and if Emma hadn't stopped smoking entirely, at least she'd cut back to one or two a day. Ben Leonard had contrived to bump into Garry Wheelan in Angel Row library and convinced him that talking to one of the doctors at the Priory about his recurring headaches and insomnia might not be a total waste of time.

Too good to last?

Whitemore was relaxing at home, the end of a not too stressful day, a small glass of whisky by his side, Glenmorangie, single malt; one of his father's old albums on the turntable — Armstrong, the Hot Sevens — when the phone called him back across the room. A domestic, Forest Fields, one of his.

By the time he arrived there were two police cars and an ambulance, beat officers doing their best to keep a conglomeration of gawkers at bay.

The front room was a disaster, the kitchen little better. Sticks of broken furniture, curtains torn down and ripped across, shredded cushions, shattered plates and mugs; the television set lay in the centre of the floor, screen splintered across. Only the framed photographs of Jade and her brothers seemed to have survived unscathed, perched precariously on the shelf above the fireplace, looking on.

Jade herself was in the back of the ambulance, being treated by one of the paramedics for a cut on her forehead, where she had been struck by flying glass.

Emma was sitting on the stairs, heavily pregnant, half-dazed, a cigarette burning away between her fingers, all but forgotten. After talking to the officers who had responded to the call, Whitemore squeezed himself onto the stairs beside her; took the smouldering cigarette from her hand and stubbed it out on the sole of his shoe.

"What happened?"

He had to ask several times before she replied.

"I dunno, he just... he just went mad, really mad, lost it, lost it altogether."

"Garry?"

"Garry. Screaming an' shoutin'. Throwing things. Smashing furniture. Everything. Took hold o' me at, didn't he? Lifted me up in the air... I thought, I dunno what I thought... pissin' meself, I don't mind tellin' you. Thought he was gonna say somethin' but he never did.

27

Just sort of stared then put me back down, careful, careful as you like. Walked out. Jade was cryin', blood runnin' down her face and cryin'. Cryin' for him to come back. Mad bastard, he never did. I hope he never does."

"What started it?" Whitemore asked. "Kicked it all off?"

Emma shook her head.

"We was just sittin' there, normal like, you know? I'd not long made us a cup of tea. Some rubbish on the telly. Garry, he was quiet, yeah, but no quieter'n usual. I s'pose I might have been talking 'bout the baby. Talking too much, maybe. Silly stuff, really. Then it kicked, really hard, you know, the baby, and I said somethin' like, here Garry, feel that, an' took hold of his hand and put it there — here — like I'd done before, plenty of times, but this time..."

Whitemore thought she was about to cry, but instead she looked down at her empty hand.

"Don't s'pose you've got a cigarette, have you?"

A sliver of moon slipped out from behind a cloud then disappeared: the sky over the city never really dark, a persistent orange glow. Whitemore could just distinguish the shape, hunched forward, face lost in shadow. The same bench as before.

Wheelan scarcely looked up as Whitemore approached, sat down.

"How is she? Emma?"

"Pretty much as you'd expect. Uncomprehending. Frightened."

"And the girl?"

"Bar a couple of stitches, she'll be okay."

"Thank Christ."

"It could've been worse."

"Think I don't know that?"

Something scuttled along the hedgerow at their backs. Whitemore was conscious of the other man's breathing, his proximity, the sudden movement of his foot as it scraped against gravel and then was still.

Minutes passed. More.

Voices, sudden and raucous, from the far side of the park.

The occasional car passing along Waverley Street towards the Forest.

"Helmand," Wheelan said suddenly. "We were in Helmand. Nahr-e Saraj. Lost someone there to snipers the day before. Out on patrol. Three days before it had been an IED. Two seriously wounded, one trapped inside. It was a bad time.

"We'd had intelligence of Taliban holed up in a building that had been a school. Before the Taliban shut it down. Went in at night. Not like this. Real night. Stars and fuck all else. Best chance of taking the bastards by surprise.

"I was in the lead group, two in front, Preston and Jagger, me and McQuaid close behind. Couple of stun grenades and then we're in, hollering at the tops of our voices, all bloody hell breaking loose, automatic fire from the top of the stairs. 'Left, left!' McQuaid shouts, pointing, and I'm ducking low, pushing through into this room, and as soon as I'm inside there's movement along the side wall, hands raised as if holding a weapon, and I'm firing, two bursts and then a third to be sure, over before it's begun, and then a light over my shoulder and I can see what I've done.

"The boy was maybe eight or nine, no older, a good half of his face gone missing. The girl was younger, four or five at most, some kind of doll clutched fast against her night-shirt with both hands. Except it wasn't a doll.

"'Jesus fuck!' McQuaid said over my shoulder. 'Get the fuck out of here now.'

"Searched the place from top to bottom. No hidden weapons and if the Taliban had been there, they were on their toes before we arrived. Before heading back to camp, we called in an air strike, blew the place to the ground."

When Whitemore shivered he tried to tell himself it was the cold.

"That's what you see?" he said. "In your dreams?"

"In my dreams they're still alive, still breathing. Hold out their hands towards me, speak in a language I don't understand. If I help them I can stop them dying. The girl, she looks a bit like Jade, but younger."

He got to his feet.

"Some time when Emma's not around, I'll get my stuff."

"You sure?"

"What was it you said before? The appropriateness of any relationships she may have formed? I think we both know the answer to that."

Whitemore watched him walk away, head down, dissolving into the pattern of the surrounding trees.

Emma's baby was born at four in the morning after a prolonged labour, a dark-haired, dark-eyed girl weighing six pounds, nine ounces. Jade was delighted with her new baby sister, Emma exhausted. Whitemore let Garry Wheelan know as promised and three days after mother and baby returned home, a parcel arrived with a West Midlands postmark, a rag doll with a pink dress and ribbons in her hair wrapped in tissue paper, and a card offering congratulations. Unsigned.

"This'll be from your dad," Emma said, "More than likely." And she lay the doll carefully down alongside the baby.

# Here We Are Again
## Megan Taylor

My train arrives so late that I'm not sure if you will be there. I hurry anyway; we don't stop to say hello to the geese on the canal or to stare into any of the glossy new shops, but with the heat on my neck and Emily's squirming, it still seems to take forever to push the buggy from the station. By the time we reach the Square, the handles are sticking to my palms, my T-shirt's slicked to my back and Emily's whining is threatening to spill over into full-blown sobs.

"It's OK." I try to sound bright. "Here we are again!" But the Square wavers; it's all silvery angles and dizzying crowds.

The sun appears to have dragged out the entire city and judging by the expressions on the sweaty faces floating by, I'm not the only one who's dazed. Everywhere, there are splashes of surprised-looking skin, hiked-up skirts and rolled-back cuffs, coats carried resentfully in bundles. Complete strangers smile as if in shock.

Crossing the road, I wonder if I'm smiling too. I'd like you to see me smiling, but my head's crackling with exhaustion. The tram tracks flare, and there's more light glittering from the paving stones ahead; the concrete looks woven through with tinsel. Even the old domed council building shines: a creamy glow to its stone columns and lions.

I don't expect you to be waiting with the lions. At twenty-two, we're already too old to be hanging out with the Goth-kids and the punks and emos, and even they seem to have moved on. They're no longer gathered en masse, at least not today, but scattered among the ordinary suits and skirts and trainers so there's just a glimpse now and then of turquoise hair, a glint of clunky buckled boots.

Still, it's enough to bring back the purple lipstick that we used to share, the belly piercing I talked you into. The tattoo parlour, not far from here, where I helped you unbutton your skirt because your hands were shaking, where the angled lamp burned a line along the rise of your hip —

"Mum-mum!"

Emily is shouting, chanting; she's forgotten that she's cross: "*Mum-mum-mum.*" She's straining at the buggy straps, her dark eyes glimmering — but it takes me a few seconds to follow her gaze and then to register the fountains. A flickering tunnel of manufactured rain, spouting laughter and diamonds, flooded with kids.

"OK," I say, "why not?"

It's as good a place as any, I suppose, in which to watch for you, to wait.

I push our way over, past a group of women with leaflets and boys with skateboards, a long row of blondes perched on a granite block. "Excuse me," I say, "excuse me, please." I dodge face after face; not one of them is yours.

At the fountains, Emily tugs at her straps and then clenches her fists, grasping at the warm air as if she can

32

use it to heave herself free. As soon as I've unclipped her from the buggy, she's off, bounding straight towards the splashing, screaming kids.

They're like a pack of puppies, out there, shaking the beads of water from their hair and snapping at them, catching the silvery drops on their bright pink tongues. They all look so happy; for a moment, I consider slipping off my shoes and joining them.

If you were here, maybe I would.

But you are not here.

*You are not here* — and maybe the best thing for me to do is to sit down with all the other mothers as if I'm no different from any of them? I'll pretend I'm not waiting for anything except for my child to finish playing, that I'm simply killing time.

But the other mothers are lined up along their own concrete block, watching their kids, or half-watching them, texting and chatting: a wall of crossed legs and rummaged handbags. I have to force myself over, dragging the buggy awkwardly behind me and it's all "Excuse me, excuse me," again before I finally find a space to sit. As I squeeze in beside a woman in a lime-coloured vest, I narrow my eyes against the day's glare and try to focus only on Emily; she's clapping water and laughing. I won't check my phone again — I *won't*.

But what if that last text didn't send? The reception's so dodgy on the train, the signal fluttering the entire way; there were long moments when I felt like I was trapped in that carriage, the journey like some recurring dream...

It never used to feel like that. When I started travelling up here to visit my dad, I was only fourteen and mostly excited. I'd spend much of the train ride swaying in the toilets, scrawling on black eyeliner... By the time I turned fifteen, it was you who would come to meet me from the station. Dad never minded; he was often busy, and the fact that I'd become such close friends with the young girl who lived on his street helped to make the separation easier, our visits smoother.

You'd shriek my name before I'd even stepped on to the platform. Then you'd throw your arms around me and drag me off to the Ladies, where we drew our eyeliner on all over again and you'd gabble about the plans you'd made for us. There would always be some party or another to go to, or an undercover pub mission. At the very least, there would be some boys for me to meet — cider in the graveyard, spliffs in the woods...

Maybe it was because I was from London that you thought I needed something extra, something shinier — flashy new risks. And maybe I liked it that you thought that, the idea that it was you who was following me?

I never told you about the times I felt like a ghost next to you. Peering through the smears in the station mirror, your hair was so much thicker, your face fuller. Even your lips were plumper than mine — though you'd say, over and over, how you wished that you were thin, like me. "No," I'd reply, just "no." I couldn't explain how you were so much more real.

Now you've grown long and willowy, comfortable in your flesh. I've seen your pictures on the internet, how confident you look — while I have stretch-marks and a Caesarean scar. And some days, the whole of my skin feels tired...

The phone is back in my hand, despite myself. There are no new messages.

I glance quickly over to the fountains — and see that Emily, at least, has found a friend. A child about the same size as her, though her wet hair's a shade paler, sequinned with light. The pair of them are drenched, stilled momentarily beneath a starry bridge of falling water. Their hands are cupped together, catching the twinkles as if they're fairies; they look very serious, watching them dance.

My throat closes. A tram clangs and I turn towards it before it heads off towards the theatre and the universities, sliding up the hill to the Arboretum —

Would you have been waiting if I'd suggested meeting there?

On a sunny day like today, the Arboretum will be at its best, all trilling birdsong and frothy blossom. We used to hang out there a lot. At first, there were just the two of us; we'd go there to chat; sometimes we'd even bring bread for the ducks. Later on though, there was beer, and then spirits and pills and a whole gang of boys. It's where I lost my virginity after a game of spin-the-bottle — you *must* remember.

It was mid-August, that spin-the-bottle night, proper summer, but there was an underlying chill to the air. While much of that evening has been smudged out long ago, that's one of the things I remember clearly. How, after the boy had left me, I lay beneath the deepening sky and started to shiver, a thin cold creeping over my skin where it was bared. I'd wanted to pull on my jacket; I'd wanted to wrap myself up, but the jacket had been crushed underneath me and was probably stained. For a long time I didn't dare to move. I just shut my eyes and listened to the leaves whispering, and finally you came for me, exactly as I'd hoped.

But that was also the night I started lying to you. When you asked me if I was OK, I said that everything was cool; we were cool and the boy was cool... And in the days, the weeks, the months that followed, there were more lies and another boy, and then another, and then it was me who was dragging you off to parties, drinking and smoking more than I'd ever done before.

But however bad I got, you kept on being there. You'd bundle me into cabs and make up excuses for my Dad. You held back my hair when I threw up. And while you stopped trying to keep up with me, you didn't judge me either. Other people had their theories — I was trying to shake off some posh-little-girl image or reacting belatedly to my parents' divorce... But you never said anything, although there were moments, many moments, when I wished that you would.

Obviously, it's madness to blame you for those blurry years — you'd never have guessed what I was really fighting, how hard it had become for me to see you without a bottle of cider between us or a joint in my hand. And all those boys...

You never once saw through it to the desperation. You'd never have imagined how frightened I was or that I thought I had anything to prove.

Do you even remember that night, that spinning bottle, the boys whooping and leering? Shouting because they thought it was hilarious that the girls had ended up with one another... Do you remember pushing the crumpled cans out of your way? How you crawled towards me across the grass...

Most likely, you've forgotten it. It wasn't something we even laughed about afterwards. You didn't care —

A part of me blames you, still.

But these are my night thoughts; they don't belong out here with the sunshine and the fountains, with my daughter kicking up rainbows, her hands held high. These are thoughts for the darkest hours when I can't find sleep even after Emily has, terrible moments when I pace the stripes on my bedroom rug and wonder what life would be like if I'd had the abortion after all. If we hadn't run from the clinic, hand-in-hand, after you told me that I didn't have to go through with it if it wasn't what I wanted, that I could do *anything*... Even then, your faith in me unwavering, though I'd never, or almost never, felt so scared.

How different would things be if I'd never had to visit that clinic in the first place, if the pregnancy test had revealed one line instead of two... In a different past, maybe I wouldn't have gone with that boy in the Arboretum; I might not have gone with any of those boys. I could have studied at university, just like I was meant to — just like you did. In another world, maybe we haven't even met...

Shadow-thoughts, they circle pointlessly, and on the worst nights, I'll stop my pacing. I open my laptop instead to look at your photographs all over again, to check on your status... For a long time, secretly, it has been me who has been following you.

I've watched your pictures change, your hair cropped short and then growing out again, bleached and then dyed orange before fading back to you. I've studied your different clothes, your varying styles, the fluctuations in your weight before it settled. I've seen your uni-friends, their stupid, laughing faces crowding close, too close, at parties and on picnics, in the glow of a barbecue, on a wide gold beach... And how easily, I've thought, everything has come to you. I've seen your girlfriends too.

While my world has narrowed, I've watched yours grow. Your whole life opening wide across my blue-lit screen, while the darkness piles up around me, my little bedroom, heaped with dirty washing. The dawn, when it arrives, a thick grey weight...

But here is my daughter, sitting down now, with her new friend. They're giggling again, trailing their fingers through the water, connecting the rivulets, spreading the gloss. I take in the silk of her damp skin and the small, pink 'o' of her mouth, and I think how if anyone were to ask, I'd tell them she's worth it. That, despite the exhaustion and endless worries, I don't regret a single thing —

I wonder if you know that's not quite true. Maybe you understand everything about me — and that's why you're not here.

*You are still not here.*

The Council House bell starts to chime and I know that you're not coming, that I was mad to ever think you would. Mad to have come back here myself, to buy a ticket I couldn't afford and then to phone Dad to tell him that Emily and I would be staying, as if it was normal to arrange it like that, out of nowhere. All because two sleepless nights ago I'd seen your update on the internet: *Single again! I'm going home!!*

And I'd thought that maybe home wasn't a place, but a person. I'd hoped for far too much.

I should go.

It'll be Dad kept waiting at this rate, and I still have him, I suppose. Never mind his disappointment and his impatience, the way that whenever Emily cries, he tries not to flinch...

She might well cry now, when I go to fetch her. Wrenched from her playground, there's the possibility of a full blown tantrum, a proper mardy. She might kick her feet and toss her head, screaming back to the friend she'll be leaving behind.

Too bad, I think, *too bad.*

I stand and stamp free the brake on the buggy, but when I look back up, through the shimmering spray, you're there —

And everything rushes towards me, the whole bright city. Not just the Square, with its people and lions and glittering stone, but the parks where we would drink and the station where we'd meet. The Arboretum, where we played a stupid game one night, where you came crawling towards me across the grass.

Crawling towards me, with your dark eyes shimmering. Your purple lipstick smudged even before you pressed your mouth to mine —

Coming towards me, right now, dressed in a smart beige suit, your hair pinned back as if you're a grown-up, though it's spilling down one side —

38

And with the memory of a spinning bottle, a single kiss, the terror comes back too. The fear that made me push you away. When I turned to a boy, that night, to all of those boys, because I could hardly look at you after you kissed me. I was so scared that I might break...

But you're walking closer, spreading your arms like wings as you step straight through the fountains.

"Here we are again!"

I think that's what you're saying, but it's a struggle to hear over the tumble of water and my daughter's laughter. And I'm also laughing, I realise, laughing so hard that my eyes are stinging. But your arms are open and as I step into them, I'm not worrying about how late it might be or about what might come next.

*Here we are again.* Here you are, right here — and maybe that's enough to make me brave? To lift my hands to your face and kiss you, though I can't see your expression. There's all this light.

# Simone
# the Stylite
*Brick*

The solo voyager

the dogged explorer

the lone wolf

the push against the shoves.

*Now we're the freaks*    *the deviants*    *the sociopaths*    *the psychokillers.*

*Okay, we aren't like the other 'outsiders'...*

Just flip it open an' push rod t' lock it.

*the gays, Muslims, immigrants, trainspotters... (how long have you got?).*

Goin' climbin'?

THUNK

Just for an hour.

*So I like my own company.*

*Is that so threatening?*

Awwh, m'boyz!

44

It's got so's...

In fact, I like people, honestly... in their place.

I have a partner, sure, and a little lad...

And I work in an office of eight on a team of twenty...

CITY

Burton Joyce

And can be quite the live wire.

Office dos? Don't do 'em. I work for the company to source money...

Not company.

'Course I have friends, a precious few. They're dear to me, so dear I have to save up to treat myself...

And I make every mouthful count.

49

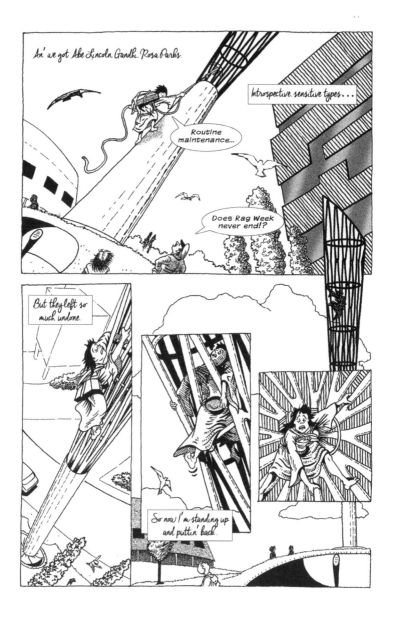

50

51

53

It's seasonal. In summer we employ extra staff, but it's fully costed.

And the Favella?

You mean Camp Simone?

Some would say a few of our buildings are more so.

Bit of an eye-sore?

But you allow it?

It's not an Occupy protest or pilgrim's camp. Only Simone's son and partner are resident.

Anybody can apply for a pitch, but just for a week. In payment, they give a talk, so every evening our marquee offers something from the street for students, staff and public.

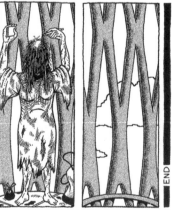

With apologies to Brian Eno & Peter Schmidt

# A Foreign Land
*Paula Rawsthorne*

Oh my God! I don't believe it! Mrs Arnold has chained herself to the gates. They're shouting at one of the guards, telling him to get cutters. They can't get us out of this place with her there. She's mad, Mrs Arnold! She's like seventy-something and she acts like one of those gorilla fighters; like that Che bloke on the T-shirts only without the cool beret, although Mrs Arnold does have a bit of a moustache.

Mum said Mrs Arnold had never been in trouble until she met us. Mum begged her to stop after the arrest, but she wouldn't. The first time they tried to get us at the flats, Mrs Arnold spotted them parking their vans, so by the time they'd reached the Tower she'd got loads of people blocking the entrance. Even from the tenth floor I could hear all the aggro. The police got a right shock.

All these people shouting at them.

"Leave the family alone."

"You're a bunch of bastard child snatchers."

"You should be ashamed of yourselves."

"Why aren't you out catching criminals instead of kidnapping innocent people?"

It was brilliant! They had this big stand-off for ages. The police gave up eventually but said they'd be back, so the next time they came, Mrs Arnold slashed the tyres on their vans; that's when they arrested her, that's when she got the local news involved.

We all went round her flat to watch her on the telly. It was like a party. The place was packed and everyone had brought food and drink. Me and Amira stuffed ourselves. It was great.

I didn't recognise her on the telly, at first. She looked so old, like a real coffin dodger. She was all bent over, shuffling with a stick; which was really weird because my Mum says, since Mrs Arnold has been getting in trouble with the police she looks twenty years younger. Anyway, turns out it was all an act. Her solicitor told her to look as ill and granny-like as possible and, when Mrs Arnold saw herself on the telly, she laughed so much that I reckon she near *wet herself.*

She got off with a fine and she only had to pay a pound a week — even I could do that! And there was a big cheer when they interviewed her outside the court. I don't know whether she'd rehearsed it or what cos I never knew that she could talk like that, but she sounded brilliant, like she was in some movie. She looked straight into the camera, all watery-eyed and said, "I'm a law-abiding grandmother but I will not sit back and watch while they try to drag a lovely, decent family out of their home and force them back to a country where they face danger and persecution. The Aziz family are an important part of our community. They've lived here for six years. Their children, Jamal and Amira, can only remember this country as their home. I'm sure that our local M.P., Andrew Cotter, will help to ensure that this family can remain here despite the inhumane decision to reject their appeal."

How good was that! It would've been great going into school cos I could've been famous for the day. All my class would love to be on the telly, and I was... kind of. Anyway, I bet Miss Rogers will talk about it to them, cos she was always dead nice to me. Not because she feels sorry for me or anything; it's cos I make her laugh. She said she could see me on the stage when I was older. She said to me, "Jay, you could be the Sudanese Peter Kay."

I've always had the top bunk and Amira's in the bottom. It bugs me because she has all her stupid dolls and teddies all over the place so it's good that my proper mates don't come round. There's another Beri family in our Tower and Dad used to always invite their son round to play with me. Dad wanted us to be friends. I felt sorry for the lad and everything but there's no way we were going to be friends. He can't even speak English and I've tried my best to forget all that Zaghawa stuff, even though Dad tried to make us speak it at home. The lad's in my year at school and at play time he just walks round with the mid-day supervisor! We've got quite a few asylum seeker kids at my school. You'd think that they'd all hang round together seeing as no one else talks to them but they don't, because most of them can't talk to each other neither.

There are some kids from my school live here but none of them are my *good* mates. My real mates aren't allowed to come to mine. They say that their mums say that the Tower Estate is too rough. But that's better, because, to be honest, I don't want them seeing what a dump I live in and it means that I can tell them that I've got an X-box and they'll never know I'm lying, so it works out okay, really.

My best mate is Eddie, but he isn't allowed to come to mine neither, but I get to go round his house loads and his mum and dad are always dead nice to me. Although his mum does talk to me like I've got special needs but I can put up with that because they take me to the Forest games and, after, we go to Pizza Hut. It's *well* good! Eddie even wanted me to go on holiday with them to Spain the other summer but it turned out I couldn't because I haven't got my passport so I'm not allowed to leave the country which is weird because from what the posters round the estate say, you'd think people would be happy if we left the country.

Eddie is such a top mate that he even gave me his old mobile; said he was fed up of not being able to get hold of me. We still haven't got a phone in the flat, even though we've been here forever. Mum reckons we were lucky; this is the first place they put us after we arrived in England. But when Mum and Dad brought us here, they didn't have any stuff with them. Uncle Osman told me that.

Mum and Dad don't talk about it but Uncle says that I'm a little man now and I should know about 'my home-land'. He's told me about that President wanted for war crimes against 'my people' and about the Janjaweed, 'devils on horseback', he calls them. He said they've burnt down all the villages and murdered thousands of people. He gets all stressed and starts shouting about 'Government-backed genocide' — whatever that means. He says it's been going on for years and all the world knows about it but does nothing... I don't know what to say to him, so I don't say anything. But I've seen it on the news, anyway. It looks like one massive campsite in a desert, but with no water and no toilets and all these skeleton people trying to keep out of the sun. And the kids look like me, only starved and half dead and there's always flies on their snot — it's gross. Darfur, 'my home-land'? They can keep it!

Dad used to say that when we know we can stay here forever, then he'll be able to get a job, which he could do, no problem, because my Dad is dead clever. Back in Sudan he was a science teacher; the head of department at some big school. And once he could start earning money everything will get better. He'd say we'd move out of the Tower Estate and rent a nice house somewhere close to our school and he'd be able to buy us nice things and there'd be no more living off charity and having to accept hand-outs... but he stopped saying stuff like that a long time ago.

I know it's not nice to say this about your own Dad, but he's become *well* embarrassing. He goes round with loads of clothes on. He wears a bobble hat all the time — he looks like some mental, homeless guy. Mum tries to keep him smart, tries to get him interested in things, but every day he's sad. He stopped taking me to mosque ages ago, which is fine by me, but he used to go all the time and when I talk to him, he's not really listening; he looks right through me. He's got *hundreds* of tablets off the doctor. I've seen them by his bed. He shouldn't take them, cos they just make him even more of a zombie.

He used to do loads with us. Over the summer holidays he'd organise all the days out; nothing great like Alton Towers, but we still had a good laugh. A load of families from the Tower would go to Wollaton Park and we'd spend all day playing footie and cricket and running round the hall looking at the stuffed animals. Some of the girls would say, "Ohh, it's so cruel to stuff the animals." And I'd say, "What's your problem? They were dead anyway."

Dad used to walk with me into town and tell me about things. I remember the first time he took me to see the castle. I couldn't believe it; it didn't look anything like the one in the movie. There were people dressed up and everything, but I saw Friar Tuck behind a tree, smoking, and Robin Hood was on his mobile swearing at someone about money they owed him. Me and Dad had a real laugh that day, but you can't have a laugh with him any more. When we'd go off to school, he'd be in bed and when we got back, he'd *still* be in bed. What he needs is some mates, like my Mum; she's got loads. Mrs Arnold was the first person she met when we came here. I can't really remember cos I was only four but Mum says Mrs Arnold was very kind to us. My Mum found her scrubbing our door because someone had written something bad on it and Mrs Arnold said to her, "Don't you worry, duck. We're not all ignorant scumbags here." Uncle Osman told me that.

Mum loves it here. Well... I suppose she doesn't love the damp patches in the flat and the having no money and the druggies on the stairs, but she just seems happy. Sometimes you can't move in our flat for all the girls with their babies. Mum helps them study for their GCSE English. They're meant to go to a special mother and baby unit in town but they can't be bothered, but they don't mind staying on the estate and having lessons and she lets them smoke as long as they put their heads out of the windows. My Mum speaks better English than any of them. She teaches them all the stuff she taught in Sudan. Last year five of them passed and one of them, Tiffany, got into college. Mum was *well* happy, it was like she'd got into Oxford or something.

Then there's 'The Ladies of the Tower Book Group'. Mum and Mrs Arnold started that. For ages it was just the two of them but then more women came along and once a month they meet in each other's flats and talk about books. It sounds dead boring to me but that's not all that they do because sometimes Mum comes back giggling, with her head scarf on wonky and Dad used to tut and get a bit mardy, but Mum would say. "I'm only 'integrating into the community'. Isn't that what our case worker told us to do?"

I got home from school, just before the Christmas holidays, and there was a hole in the kitchen wall. I said to Mum, "Why's there a hole in the wall?" And she said "Oh, it was a silly accident."

She must think I'm stupid. I saw Dad's hand. It was all swollen and bruised. It's not like he's Superman or anything. The walls in our flat are like cardboard. I wouldn't let it drop but mum *still* lied to me. She thinks I'm a little kid and won't be able to handle stuff. It's Amira who's the little kid — she's only seven, but I'm ten. I'm in Year Six, not foundation!

Mum was all stressed after the hole in the wall day. She pretended not to be and she tried to make Christmas fun but she was always going out to meetings. And I kept thinking, 'Since when did Mum have meetings?' But then, for ages, everything seemed to be normal and I forgot about it until, one morning, this letter arrived and I'm not joking, it was like getting the Black Spot in *Treasure Island* because, after that, everything went *really, really bad*. Mum started having hysterics and Dad was sat there, staring into space. I didn't know what to do so I ran and got Uncle Osman and he came round and told me and Amira to stay in our room and play but I could hear everything. They were talking Zaghawa but I could understand a lot of it. Uncle was saying that we should go into hiding so that they couldn't send us back, and Dad was mumbling about not being criminals. But Uncle started shouting, telling Dad he was a fool. He told them about a man who was sent back the other week; a farmer from south Darfur, been here for three years. Uncle said the bastards murdered him even before he made it out of Khartoum airport. He said that no one going back was safe. He said that Darfur was a living hell that the world had forgotten about. He said, that in Khartoum, our people had been shot in the streets and that everything was even worse than when those men grabbed Mum in the streets of Omdurman and told her they'd burn us to death while we slept.

I sat on the bunk bed, shaking. I thought I was going to throw up. I looked down at Amira. She was just playing with her dolls, singing a stupid song. Why hadn't Mum gone to the police when those men said those things to her? They must have police even in a place as rubbish as Sudan. Why didn't she get them arrested? And if Mum told our case worker about this then why would they be telling us to go back? Anyway, we've been here so long I thought we were British now. I thought they must have made a mistake. I reckoned Mum and Dad could speak to the case worker woman and sort it out.

After that letter came, Mum said we shouldn't go to school for a while and a few weeks later Miss Rogers came round with *homework* for us. I was a bit gutted but I suppose it was nice of her. When she was leaving she hugged Mum and said that the school had started a petition to give to our M.P. Mum just started crying and then things got really weird cos Miss Rogers kissed me. Actually kissed me! On the cheek! I was dead embarrassed... she smelled lovely though.

It was horrible when the social worker came round. Mum wouldn't have opened the door but she'd been expecting Mrs Arnold. She told Mum that she'd come to have a chat. Mum made us sit on her knee even though I'm too old to do stuff like that, but she put her arm around me to make me stay.

The lady smiled at us a lot but really she was dead serious and kept saying sorry to Mum. She was saying stuff about me and Amira, now that all our benefits had been stopped. She was saying that she could see that we were very well looked after but how long could that continue with no money. Going on about us being 'at risk'.

"At risk of what?" I asked.

"Well, Jamal," she started all soft-like.

But I told her, "My name's Jay."

"Well, Jay, it's complicated," she said.

"No it's not," I said. "Just let us stay and let my Dad get a job so he'll be able to buy things. Why are you making us go back? I don't even know the place and there's these people over there who are going to *kill* us, you know, and it'll be your fault!"

Mum started crying and telling me to shush, that I was being silly and frightening Amira.

The lady spoke to Mum. "I've got nothing to do with your asylum application. My concern is your children's welfare now that your appeal has been rejected. I'm sorry, I really am, but unless you agree to return to your country, we will be forced to look at instigating care proceedings."

\*\*\*

Last week, when they came to our flat to get us, I nearly had a heart attack. At first, I thought we were being robbed! The front door was smashed open and then these men came into our bedroom, switched the light on and said, "Please get up."

I didn't know if they were the social workers or the immigration lot but Amira was still half asleep and was screaming like she was being murdered or something. Mum ran in and tried to calm her down. It all happened so quick. I grabbed my phone from under the pillow and they gave Mum five minutes to pack some clothes for us all. Mum was shouting at them saying, "At least let us get dressed!"

They didn't shout back, they just towered over her and said that they were sorry but we had to come with them immediately.

And do you know what Dad did? Nothing! Absolutely nothing! He stood there as if it wasn't even happening. And next minute they were hassling us towards the lift and our neighbours were opening their doors, looking out. That's when Patrick saw me. Patrick's in Year Six as well, but he's not my mate. He's from the Congo. He's well 'ard! He goes round school saying that he was in the army and he's killed people. I know he's lying cos they don't let kids in the army, but he's a psycho, anyway. And he saw me being marched out, wearing *Ben 10* pyjamas. He'll tell all the kids at school that I wear *Ben10* pyjamas. But I don't, it's just Mum makes me, because we got given them and Mum says we should be grateful for what we get.

Mrs Arnold came running down the corridor in her nightie. She didn't even have her teeth in and she was screaming at the men but one of them waited behind and wouldn't let her pass. It was still dark outside. It was three o'clock in the morning — I checked on my phone. They put us in the back of this van. It didn't even have windows.

***

It's not just Mrs Arnold here. I can see other neighbours *and* Uncle Osman outside the detention centre. They've even made signs. They must have come in the community minibus. I'm surprised it made it all the way here, cos it didn't even make it to Skeggy that time without breaking down. We got there in the end though and it was a well good day! We had ice creams and candy floss and I soaked Amira in the sea. The sea was miles out. It took ages to get to it and it rained, but it was still great.

I recognise all of them. There's a couple of Mum's girls with their babies and there's the nice family from Syria — they live down our corridor and Mum's book group and that lady with the son in prison, even though he's innocent — they had him on CCTV robbing a jewellery shop but she says 'it's a case of mistaken identity'. Anyway, I'm glad they're here. They all look knackered.

Mrs Arnold is shouting to Mum. "Local news can't make it. I tried, but Katie Price is doing a book signing in

66

the Vicky Centre. They said they didn't have a spare camera crew. I've left a dozen messages for Andrew Cotter, but he hasn't got back to me yet. *Evening Post* said they'd print something, though. So at least that's one thing. Loads more people wanted to come but we didn't have the space."

Mrs Arnold isn't looking at Dad. I know why. She's *really* angry with him. She reckoned that if we just stayed in other people's flats then the immigration people would never catch us. She'd made up a rota of the families who'd said that we could bunk down at theirs. But Dad wasn't having any of it. He said that he wasn't going to live like that.

The security guard has cut through Mrs Arnold's chains. They drag her out the way and open the gates. Everyone rushes towards us, but the men hold them back. Uncle Osman looks like he wants to beat them up, but he's got no chance — these blokes are massive! I bet they're on steroids! We did about them in our Drug Awareness lessons — it's not worth it — they make your willy shrivel up.

Uncle Osman is shouting to us, "We'll get you back. We won't give up."

Mrs Arnold's nodding so hard her head's going to fall off. "Yeah, you're not to worry, Rashida. And I'll come visit you; bring my bikini. Give those Muslim Brothers something to look at."

Mum laughs but she's crying and they push us past everyone.

***

There's Eddie! I don't believe it! He's here, with his Mum and Dad. We've been phoning each other. I told him they were going to make us go on a plane to Sudan. I didn't think he'd come. He's got a brilliant car though — BMW 3 Series Convertible. Bet they got here well before the minibus. His Mum's looking at me like I'm a puppy about to be put down. I wish she'd just smile or something.

He shouts at me. "Ey up, Jay."

"Ey up, Eddie." I say

"It's bad all this innit?" he says

"Yeah, it's not good."

"Text me?"

"Sure. Soon as I get there." I reply. But really I'm thinking — what are the chances of getting a signal in a place like Sudan? They haven't even got proper loos.

He chucks his Forest scarf to me.

"Cheers, Eddie," I say, "but I don't think I'll need it; it's 50 degrees out there." I should have been pleased with that, because it's quite a funny thing to say, but I can feel myself about to cry and I bite the inside of my cheek because I don't want him to see me blubbing, but I don't think I can stop it. I can feel tears rolling down my face and I want to hide it but I can't properly cos Mum's got hold of my hand. And Amira's holding her other hand and my head is banging cos Amira hasn't stopped wailing since they took us from the flat. And Dad's just walking ahead of us, carrying the bags. He hasn't said a word. I don't know what's going on inside his scrambled egg brain, but how's he going to protect us from those people when he's like he is? They might be waiting at the airport for us, like they were for that man.

I can see the plane, there's already people on it. They must be waiting for us. And Mum starts talking, all sing-song like.

"Isn't this exciting? You're going to see your home at last. We'll be able to see your Uncles and Aunties and there'll be new cousins to play with and lots of new friends. We'll be able to show you Jebel Marra and in Khartoum we'll visit Omdurman market and you'll see where the Blue and White Nile meet. And wait until you taste proper Ful; so much better than mine." And all the time she's squeezing my hand tighter and tighter until Amira stops crying and shouts at her.

"Stop it, Mummy. You're hurting me."

But me, I'm looking at that plane, and all I can think is: 'Please, please, someone tell us that we don't have to go.' And I look back at Eddie and I know that if someone said to me right now. "Listen Jay, you belong here. You can stay. You can go and live with your mate but I'm afraid Mum, Dad and Amira have to leave." Do you know what? I love them and everything but I'd still say okay. That's what I'd say, honest. I'm disgusting, aren't I? I'm an evil little git.

But you know, I've been thinking a lot about it and really, there's no way they'd send us back if bad things were going to happen, would they? No way! I reckon that man who got killed at the airport was probably some criminal anyway and some gangster got him and those men who threatened Mum; well that was years ago, wasn't it? They're probably dead by now or they've forgotten. And Uncle Osman, well, he's *always* exaggerating stuff.

Anyway, as soon as we get there, Mum will find a way to get us back. It'll be fine; like a holiday to meet all the family I never knew I had. It'll be like that 'Who Do You Think You Are?' programme. Miss Rogers will probably make me do a boring project about it.

I walk up the steps to the plane and I can just about see Eddie jumping up and down behind the security men so I start waving my scarf at him and I scream out like Forest are about to score.

"Come on you Reds!!"

And I know, that really, there's nothing to sweat about — we'll be back home before next season starts.

# Hardanger
*Alison Moore*

Sue was in-between. No longer really a child but not quite an adult either. She was as tall as her mother but still slept with her teddy bear. She was still at school but on Fridays she went to the pub with her friends, where they drank squash and ate crisps. She had a Saturday job, and with her wages she bought jewellery made out of sweets. Her bedroom door had a sign on it saying, NO ENTRY ☠ KEEP OUT.

In her bedroom, Sue had a collection of road signs that had been brought home under cover of darkness and sneaked inside while Marlene and Bill watched the news. Marlene saw them when she hoovered — she saw the red-rimmed triangles on rusting legs, the silhouetted workmen and exclamation marks. She stood in the doorway, pushing the vacuum cleaner into the room without stepping over the boundary herself. There were letters, too, the sort that belonged on shopfronts. Sue had the curving 'S' and the vowels of her Christian name. The metal prongs of the 'U' and the 'E' looked lethal. They made Marlene think of her great-uncle who lost his eye to a garden fork, apparently. She has never been able to conceive quite *how*, quite how this could have happened,

71

and so she keeps imagining it happening in all sorts of not-quite-right ways.

Marlene imagined the holes in the road that were now missing their attendant warnings, and the businesses in whose names gaps had appeared overnight. When she asked Sue to get rid of these things, Sue expressed indignation. "My signs?" she said.

"But they're *not* yours," said Marlene. "They shouldn't be in the house."

With a dismissive gesture, Sue agreed to get rid of them. "I'll take care of it," she said. But still they remained.

"I don't know what to do with them," said Marlene to Bill, but he just shook his head and shrugged. It bothered Marlene endlessly that they were there, but she couldn't carry them — as heavy and awkward as they were — back into town. She didn't want to take them on the bus. Not knowing the best way to get rid of them, she left them where they were, in Sue's bedroom. She shut the door.

It was almost a year since Marlene and her girls had moved from the farm in the Midlands to that coastal town, to Bill's house. Marlene was still adjusting. She found it odd, to be so close to water, to the sea and the mouth of a river, and yet, out in the suburbs, to be steeped in concrete slabs and pebble dash. Her younger daughter had acclimatised quickly. Lizzy liked living near the seaside, and she liked Bill and called him 'Dad'. It had occurred to Marlene that Lizzy might be young enough not even to remember her real father in due course. Sue, on the other hand, was not even trying. She resented the move and her mother's remarriage. She did not call Bill 'Dad'. She missed the farm and her father, who used to take her out walking in the countryside, where she would fill her pockets with stones, and leaves that harboured insects, and pine cones that closed up when it was going to rain, as if they knew, like the cows lying down in the fields, like the birds flying low. She unloaded them in the kitchen, making her own nature table, and Marlene said that it was very nice, but *must* it come into the house?

There was a boy, a disarmingly beautiful boy who never quite made eye contact. He came to the house and hung around, or else he took Sue out. He was older than Sue, although still just a child himself really.

"Is she old enough," said Marlene to Bill, "for a boyfriend?"

"Do you want me to warn him off?" asked Bill.

"No," said Marlene. "Keep him close."

When Sue said that she wouldn't go with them to Norway at Easter, they said she could invite the boy, Travis, to join them.

"Sure," said Travis, when Sue asked him. "Whatever." He was sitting in Bill's armchair and spoke without looking up from the guitar at whose strings he was plucking.

"Good man," said Bill, who was sitting in the cat's place on the sofa.

Marlene took Sue late-night shopping for new clothes, going by train into Plymouth. The light was going and it had started to rain. Looking out through the window, Marlene saw a field, grey beneath the stormy sky, a wide expanse of long, dense grass rippling in the wind. Then she saw that the whole field was shifting; it was rising and falling like something alive, and she realised that it wasn't a field at all, but water, the river Plym.

In Oslo, they took photos of the docks, churches, the palace and the patrolling guards. Later, looking at the images on the screen of the camera, Marlene said, "Did we not take any family photos? We should, just to prove we were here."

73

They travelled west to the outskirts of Hardanger and unloaded the car, taking their luggage into their cabin, Travis carrying his guitar. He could not really play it but he wanted to learn, he said to Bill, because it was a good way to get girls.

In Hardanger, a district known for apple blossom and cider, fiddles and folklore, they posed for snaps in front of the mountains, first with Bill taking photos of Marlene and the three children and then with Travis taking shots of Marlene and Bill and the girls. These, thought Marlene, the ones without Travis, were the *real* family photos, the ones they would keep. The sunlight gave Sue, with her fine blonde hair, a halo, as if she were a young girl saint. *Like Joan of Arc*, thought Marlene, and then, quickly, *No, not Joan of Arc*. "Smile," said Travis, and they all smiled.

But later, when they were back at the cabin and they looked at the photos, there were only the mountains, the hard, dark lines of two imposing mountains with a V of sky between them, and in the foreground, where the four of them ought to have been, there was nothing but the Hardangerfjord. "I'm no good with technology either," said Marlene to Bill, whose pictures were not there either. "It's easily done." She had once clicked 'yes' instead of 'no' on her computer and had lost a whole day's work. It could not be got back. "A whole day's work," she had said to Bill. "A whole day wasted."

Marlene got out her watercolours and took them to the window that had the best view. In the fading afternoon light, she painted a landscape. She took great care over it but later she overheard Travis saying to Bill that the pale green-grey blur in the distance could be land or water, he couldn't tell. "When she looks at it later," he said, "will she know which it is?"

There was a cupboard full of games, and Lizzy and her parents spent a morning playing Twister, while Sue, who did not want to join in, went with Travis to a nearby market.

"What have you got there?" said Bill to Travis when they returned. "A violin?"

It was a lovely-looking thing he held, like a violin, the glossy wood decorated with black rosemaling and inlaid with mother of pearl, or bone, and at the end of it, carved into the scroll, a head — an animal or a woman, it was hard to tell from a distance.

"Do you know the local story," said Travis, sitting down and beginning to saw at the strings of his new instrument, "of Little Freddy with the Fiddle? When he played, everyone started dancing and couldn't stop."

"You won't get anyone dancing to that racket," said Bill.

"The man who sold me this said that to become a good fiddler, you must ask the *Fossegrimen* to help you, and he will, for a price."

"Who's the *Fossegrimen*?"

"A water-dwelling, fiddle-playing spirit."

"Ah," said Bill, returning his attention to the Twister board. "Well, good luck with that."

The following morning, Travis was the first to get up and by the time everyone else was awake he had already gone out.

"Where's he gone?" asked Sue. "Why has he gone without me?"

"Never mind," said Marlene brightly. "We'll have a day out together, just the family."

Sue looked at Bill and said nothing, but she sulked all the way round the cider factory and picked a fight with Marlene when Marlene said, "We'll be going home tomorrow." No, said Sue, she did not want to go, she did not want to go back to Bill's house, and she harangued her mother throughout the cider tasting.

When they returned to the cabin in the evening, they found Travis there, playing his fiddle. Perhaps, thought Marlene, the cider she had drunk at the factory was affecting her judgement, but his playing seemed quite expert now. The ancient folk music tugged at her heart and, it seemed, at her feet, because she did a quick dance in the doorway. Sue, delighted by the sight of him, started laughing and clapping. "They play the fiddle," said Travis, "when they lead a bride to church."

Bill said to him, "You've been practising. Good for you."

They put Lizzy to bed, while Travis continued to play, and then Bill shared out the cider they'd brought back and they sat around drinking and tapping their feet. Marlene fell asleep. When she woke up, it was dark and she was alone.

She found Bill asleep in his clothes in the master bedroom. Lizzy was where they'd left her, in her own bed, but Sue's bed was empty. She woke Bill up. She said, "I'm getting too old to drink like that. Where's Sue?" And as she spoke, she heard the music. It was coming from outside the house. She turned around and left the bedroom, hurrying out into the night. While Bill blinked in the darkness, Marlene followed the sound of the fiddle music that was floating through the cold night air, pursuing it down a path behind the house, running for a good half mile before coming to a sudden stop at the sight of Sue dancing at the water's edge while Travis sat beneath an apple tree playing his fiddle. Marlene opened her mouth, but nothing came out, or nothing sufficient to make Sue turn around and look at her mother before jumping into the water. She went under. Marlene shouted, "Sue!" and ran to the edge, but there wasn't an edge — she stood where the edge should have been and saw that what had surely been water was a field. She stepped onto the surface of it, staring at it, at the place into which she had just seen her daughter leap, staring at the grassed-over earth at her feet. *But it was water*, she thought. She knew it was water. She had seen it. *Wasn't it water?*

She turned to Travis. "Where is she?"

"Who?" said Travis.

"Sue, where's Sue? Where did she go?"

"You all went to sleep."

"I saw her jump into the water."

"What water?" said Travis.

"Where's Sue?" she said again, but the sounds were too soft, the 'wh' and the vowels just exhaled air and the 's' just a hiss like something punctured, and the ground was hard and cold, and Travis was still playing.

# Nimmi's Wall

*Shreya Sen Handley*

It was the first good day after a long, dank winter, so she
got out of the house early before the sun could run out on
her. Nimmi was going to do what she'd been longing to
do since she arrived in Nottingham — explore the long
garden that disappeared in a cloud at the bottom. The
empty red brick house she had moved into four months
ago was now furnished to her taste and felt like home.
But the garden in these months of incessant, icy rain and
a cold, buffeting wind had been impossible to get to
know. It had taken on an aura of mystery and become
doubly alluring in the time she'd spent looking at it from
inside the protective warmth of her new home. "A
hardier soul would have been out there exploring it
already!" she reminded herself almost every day while
looking out the tall glass windows of her living room,
past her steadily swelling reflection, into the dripping
garden beyond. But it had had little effect. If she scolded
herself often about it, she also made excuses on the
grounds that she was a tropical animal, only recently
arrived from sweltering Kolkata and exceedingly cow-
ardly when it came to cold like she'd never known before.
And besides her own get-out-there-no-don't dialogue

with herself, there was no-one to really discuss it with, much less take exploring.

A couple of Sundays in, she said to Barun, "Let's go on an adventure! We don't have to go far. Why don't we find out what's at the bottom of our garden, there always seems to be a haze hanging over it."

"I only have Sundays to rest, *Yaar,*" he replied, looking horrified, after seeming not to want to speak at all for a good few minutes. "I can run you down to the Indian community centre if you really want to go somewhere." Then reacting to the dismay, this time on *her* face, he said, "Anyway, look at you, you are now too fat to be going anywhere. Didn't Dr. Gill tell you to be careful just last week?" Having delivered what he considered the last word on the subject, he turned over and fell asleep again, filling the house with snores so loud she wondered how that could be good for her health either.

It was true that the good doctor had waggled his grandfatherly finger at her and cackled, "No more excesses!" He might have said excuses, as she indulged in many more of those, but she knew he had a tic in his turban about pregnant women and the mere hint of physical exertion. He had nothing to worry about on that account, she was not the sporty, outdoorsy type but, at the same time, there rarely was a woman who liked to poke into things more. And their never-ventured-into garden was perfect for that, verging on wild and somewhat forbidding in that it seemed to hold dusk fast in its low branches even when it was bright outside.

Today, however, was different, the first genuinely warm day she had experienced since flying from India to join her surgeon husband. A delicious golden light was oozing through the branches, like honey. If she looked closely, even from her living room window it was evident the leaves were growing back. Little green buds sprouted on every branch and shrub, the latter resembling great untidy bundles of twigs left behind by some forgetful gardener all these winter months. The squelchy, grey-brown ground she'd got used to appeared green and springy, inviting her to sink her feet into it. But best of all, the perpetual fog at the bottom of the garden seemed to be lifting, leaving wispy traces dancing in the light, promising untold delights once it cleared. Nimmi stood on the back doorstep for a second letting the sun warm her shoulders in a gentle reassurance that it meant to be around for a while, at least till she finished exploring her enticing garden. She put the umbrella she thought she should have with her (on the evidence of preceding weeks) in the crook of her arm and sailed forth.

"I need to find someone to help me bring this under control," she mumbled as she went in deeper. Gorgeous was the word for this garden. It was also the only word a big city girl could come up with in the face of so much unknown beauty. Zigzagging to avoid crushing the daffodils at her feet and the foxgloves springing from the roots of the gnarly walnut trees, she had to duck (despite her diminutive stature) to stop knocking the delicate blooms off the low-hanging branches of the cherry blossom trees. When she got to the bottom the fog wrapped round the long, low 'thing' had unfurled. What she saw then made her skin prickle with excitement. It was a wall. But no ordinary wall. Even as its stones gleamed freshly in the sun, their grooved and grained surfaces looked more ancient than anything she'd seen before. Weathered and yet standing firm. Proud and crumbling at the same time. And inviting. She touched it gingerly at first, expecting a rebuke for disturbing a thousand years of sleep. Then she giggled at her fancy and ran her hands across the stones lovingly. They seemed to respond to her, growing warm under her touch.

She knew she'd be back soon. Perhaps the very next day. With laptop in tow. If it allowed her to perch on one of the large fallen stones at its base, she could sit at its feet while she surfed for what she sensed would be its amazing history.

"I told you not to go out there!" Barun practically spat into her face, gripping her thin wrists far too tightly. "You are an Indian girl, *na*? Did your hoity toity *tyash* family never tell you that good Indian girls listen to their husbands? But then Mummy said you were no good. In fact, she said you were looj."

"Loose," she corrected under her breath out of habit and realised how terribly timed that had been when his face turned purple with wrath. She waited for something to happen. Something make or break. Almost eagerly. But he just stomped off, filling the guest bedroom that night with his vuvuzela snores.

She went down to the wall the next morning. And the morning after that. And the one after. It became a daily ritual. She did not attempt to hide it. Barun began to skip breakfast, going to the hospital earlier and earlier and coming home later. Nimmi spent happy hours in the garden as it grew greener with every passing day. Laced through the deep golden green were flowers of sumptuous ruby-red, canary and teal. And not just in the trees and bushes, every winding pathway (all of which led to the wall at the bottom) was carpeted with the same.

After months of the deepest silence, the garden had burst into song — not just birds doing their thing but a steady chirruping from a symphony of bugs, with rodents chipping in for good measure. She even heard the chatter and laughter of children, but that was impossible as their neighbours on either side had extensive, heavily wooded gardens too. And no kids. She decided it was the voice of her baby and, rather pleased with the idea, didn't wonder about it again. She would have danced through her garden every afternoon if she could, so happy was she in it, but her by-now humongous bump prevented it. It prevented a lot of things but she didn't mind, she loved her bulge, whatever her feelings for its father. *Those* she did not explore too deeply.

But if dancing was not possible, plenty else was. She started by attempting to hack back the overgrowth, but she wasn't the strongest or most knowledgeable about gardening (in fact, she was clueless) and it stayed wild. She began writing the children's book she'd thought about for years, sitting on fallen branches or further down the garden, on the loose, glowing stones at the base of the wall. She took her lunch there too, throwing the remnants to birds and squirrels when she ran out of steam. She was at that stage in her pregnancy when she was no longer sick all day but could not get much down her. It was as if the growing baby was taking over inside, leaving room for neither food nor Barun.

What she really liked doing was piecing together what she could about this beautiful garden she had acquired so serendipitously. From the Domesday Book of 1086, to medieval references to walled orchards at the heart of Sherwood Forest, to newspaper reports of Byronic duelling on the same spot several centuries later, she traced the history of her wall with glee as spring wore on.

Her expanding belly and the steadily warming sun ensured she never got too far before she fell asleep, usually under a walnut tree. Waking rather uncomfortably on hard ground one afternoon, she found a bed of fallen leaves laid out for her a few feet away. Not a mound that had gathered over time and gone dank, this was a flattened patch of carefully selected, soft, warm foliage that loving hands had brought together. The thought that someone had been right by her as she slept should have frightened her. Instead she heaved her bulk to what could only be described as a special gift and fell back to sleep.

She heard the children again, the next day. This time they were close, as if her acceptance of their thoughtful gift of a leafy bed had given them the confidence to approach her.

"There she is, Clover, can you see?"

"Yessss, she's purrrty," a little-girl voice piped up. Followed by "Shall we go to her?"

"No, not today," said the older, clearly wiser child. Then the voices drifted away. When Nimmi got to the densely wooded spot by the wall where she thought she'd heard them last, they were gone. Ostensibly, over the wall. Which was, of course, physically impossible, because though the wall was low enough to look over on her side, the drop was steep on the other, with little firm foothold to be found on its crumbling face. And where in that deep, dark woodland which blocked out everything including the modern motorway that lay beyond, could they have gone? Wistfully, she followed a mossy path on the wall with her finger. The moss had, after all, been disturbed. But it didn't answer the question uppermost in her mind — who were they?

That was the question on the tip of her tongue all through dinner but she did her best not to blurt it out amidst the boring blather about politics and doctoring which she only half listened to. And only because she liked doddering Doctor Gill. Doctor and Mrs Gill had come to dinner, along with a quite insufferable younger man Barun worked with at the hospital. His wife was there too and yet, like Nimmi, not really there. Barun graced their dinner table for the first time in a month. Nimmi didn't know whether to be pleased, or disappointed she didn't have the evening to herself — now that it was light till so late she could have her meal in the heart of the garden while its denizens hunkered down for the night. Tonight she could only look at it longingly from inside, which she must have been doing when she heard Barun say, "You are a lucky man, Rajiv. I haven't had any *rotis* made for me, or a sari worn to please me in months.

84

Ever since the weather's turned, she puts on her jeans and runs out at the first opportunity, her hair like a bird's nest. She is writing something or the other. Nothing that will get published. But *shotti bolchhi*, she is, as this arty-farty friend of mine once said, away with the fairies. All the time."

Nimmi gasped audibly. It was an entirely accurate summation but to talk about her like that in front of strangers? Did he air their dirty laundry at work too? Doctor Gill, who had been looking for a hole in the ground while Barun was mouthing off, said gently, "*Beti*, you look tired. I think we should all go now. That baby," pointing a thin finger at her minor-mountain-sized bump, "needs all the rest it can get." Then with a kindly smile, he was gone. Nimmi threw a sympathetic glance at the wife of the insufferable man whose name she couldn't recall and without further ado made her own exit through the patio doors. When she went back in an hour later, the mess from dinner was still all there for her to clear but the house was deathly still. He was spending the night else-where. It was a first. She began picking up the detritus, happy to be left to do it in peace.

\* \* \*

"Don't wake her!" said the older voice.

"But look, she's beginning to come awake."

That was true. As her eyes adjusted to the bright sun-light after the long post-lunch sleep only pregnant women can allow themselves, she saw the two children for the first time. They were the strangest looking children ever but heart-tuggingly beautiful at the same time. Perched on the wall, wearing what looked like strips of tattered cloth strung together to make capes, with dusty breeches peeping from underneath, they grinned at her with gap-toothed good humour. Then the younger one, a girl, warned, "There are Damp Worms in the soil that will get

85

into your ears if you keep sleeping on the ground. Then they will eat your brain." She said this cheerfully, clearly intending to add other happy consequences, when the older child, a little man in the making, shushed her.

"Clover only means that with a baby on the way, it's better for you to nap somewhere safe," he explained, nodding his tousled head earnestly, "and we can help you." She felt such fondness for these two little creatures, her constant companions *and* guardians from the day she'd stepped into the garden, that she was quite overcome and beamed manically in response.

Pleased she remembered their names from the exchanges she'd overheard, Nimmi ventured, "Sheply and Clover? How pleased I am to meet you! Thank you so much for looking after me, but I don't want you to go to any trouble." She held out bars of chocolate, hoping it wouldn't do any harm to their nearly-not-there teeth. With eager hands they accepted her gifts, Clover sitting as close as she could at Nimmi's side to show her gratitude. Nimmi put an arm around the girl's thin shoulders and they were away, discussing Damp Worms and their misdeeds for the rest of that enchanted afternoon. They parted with the plan of regrouping the next morning, with gardening equipment and a strategy to get the overgrowth under control.

Nimmi was late out the next morning. She had had another argument with Barun, this time about her unwillingness to have his mother over for the entire first year of their baby's life. It had brought back the morning sickness. But after hanging over the toilet bowl for an hour, she had decided the best cure for nausea would be fresh air, and plunged into the garden. She ran towards the wall, excited about seeing the children, anxious that it might never happen again. As she approached, however, she slowed down. She could hear a third voice. It was deep and gruff. Something stirred in her stomach. Was her baby responding to this voice? Or was it something deeper inside, more primal? Past the last of the cherry blossom trees she could finally see her new visitor. He was peculiarly dressed like the children, but it suited him. And there was such a strange aura about him, Pied-Piper-like. He looked like a medieval flautist might, but sturdier with sinewy arms and square, work-roughened hands hanging out of scraggly sleeves. He looked up and saw her. And the expression on his face changed in a flash from cheerfully teasing as it had been with the children to something so intense, and wolfish, that her stomach twisted and her feet tangled, nearly bringing her down.

Wondering at his effect on her, she watched him while they ate their lunch under the spreading shade of the largest walnut tree. They had spent the morning hacking back the undergrowth. Or rather he had, with help (and sometimes hindrance) from the children. They had only allowed her to fetch and carry and finally to get them some lunch from the house. The garden in the meantime was transformed into a habitable version of its riotous self, without having lost any of its magic. And all because of the man's untiring arms and flashing blade.

He had begun with a deep bow, "Edric, Madame," finishing, with a twinkle in his blue eyes, "at your service." They had all worked companionably together, whooping with joy when things went right and chortling ruefully when they didn't.

In the course of the afternoon, she found herself gravitating towards him, discovering that the right amount of shade from the sun or the exact temperature she needed to feel comfortable existed only in the spot where he worked. They ended up toiling side by side that last hour.

With the children running around and playing at the end of the day, they had time and space to talk. Like the children, his English was heavily inflected and occasionally crude but that kept her laughing even when she didn't understand it all. What she did know was that she liked how it felt when their arms brushed. When their fingertips touched and seemed to tingle. When one scrutinised the other's face thinking themselves unobserved. She was the deepest brown from the wind and the sun when she floated back into the house.

Barun was home unexpectedly early, bristling at her absence.

"Where have you been?"

"Just in the garden. Making things better," she said.

"You? Gardening? No, no, you are up to something." Then more nastily still, "You look like you've been laid."

Nimmi recoiled in horror. Then with all the pent-up bitterness of the last few months, she screamed into his face, "How would *you* even know what I look like *fucked*?"

Nimmi was relieved not to see him again that week. Life was easier without Barun's resentment marring every evening. But the shock of her quickly-disintegrating marriage had begun to take its toll.

In the time that Barun was away, only the children came to visit her. Fond as she already was of her young friends, she seized the opportunity to get to know them better. On top of the sunny smiles and questions they'd always had for Nimmi, they now began to tell her about themselves.

"Where are you from? How do you get here every day?"

"We're not from afar," said Sheply. Clover took her hand and led her to the wall.

"There's our home," she confided, stabbing her finger at the thickly wooded stretch on the other side of the wall. Darkly entwined and forbidding, like her garden had been to start with, it did not look inhabited to Nimmi. Or habitable. Clover watched her face but seeing only bewilderment, leaned over further (much too far, worried Nimmi), and demanded, "See!" Nimmi peered harder and was startled to see a settlement this time. It was as if the trees had parted to give her a better view. In an emerald-green clearing were neat wattle and daub huts with smoke rising from primitive chimneys. People in the same strung-together, scrap-like clothing as the children walked busily between these. She watched, rapt. It was straight out of her childhood picture books on Robin Hood. So exactly like she would have imagined Sherwood Forest that it unsettled her. For the first time, she was unnerved by the kids and ashamed of it.

As she watched, one figure became recognisable. "Edric!" she squeaked.

Sheply gave her a knowing glance, the nearest thing to sly on such an innocent face, and said, "It's getting dark. Go back in. Get some sleep."

"Because tomorrow we have a surprise for you, you don't want to miss!" added Clover. But Nimmi was in the mood to push for more information.

"How will you go home?" she asked again.

"Down this way, of course," Sheply admitted finally, indicating the sheer drop beyond the wall. But it wasn't till she had turned her back on them and walked a good way home that they slipped away.

The next day they were not there. But in the protected green glade where she often read or wrote was a new and wonderful offering. A deftly carved wooden swing, creaking as it gently swung back and forth in the wind. Someone had just been there tying the thick, coarse ropes firmly to the branches. Someone who had made the swing itself with his square, work-roughened hands, hanging out of scraggly sleeves. "Edric?" she called. He stepped out from behind a tree with a grin.

"Did you make this for me? It's the best thing anyone's ever given me."

"Thank you," he said, his blue eyes twinkling the way she remembered. "Not better than that though." He brushed her belly with his fingertips. It was only the slightest touch but it set her quivering within. The baby had definitely stirred too.

"It likes you." She smiled up at him. He sat down beside her, laughing that he'd made the swing especially sturdy for just such an occasion. Then he rubbed her bump almost lovingly.

"I hope you don't think I'm being forward. I am drawn to this child." And when she waited, not knowing what to say to a deeply attractive man who might not even exist, he said, "And to its mother." Then he took her hands and kissed them. She touched his coppery beard. It felt very real. She then proceeded to fulfil her mother-in-law's prophecy that she'd turn out to be 'looj', by kissing him. A long, deep, passionate kiss, a torrid, fall-off-the-swing kiss, a never-let-me-go kiss; the kind she thought existed only in romance novels. It was slow and delicious, gentle so as to not hurt the child. The intensity of their feelings communicated mainly through their eyes.

It was nearly dark and the ground cold when she said, "I must get back. Though I've never wanted to less." He got up too, wordlessly, dusk-coloured in his dun cape and breeches, merging with the darkening sky. But halfway up the path to the house, when she thought she'd lost him to the night altogether, she heard him say, "Come find me if you need me."

Barun was waiting for her in the kitchen. Spoiling for a fight, he greeted a flustered Nimmi with a rictus grin. As she sat down to catch her breath unaware of what was brewing, he moved in, pinning her down with one spindly but surprisingly strong arm. Twisting her head to one side, he scrutinised what she could only guess was beard-burn. "*Arre*, a bruise from gardening, is it?" he leered. "Or have you been making *masti* with the gardener? You've obviously acquired one. You didn't do that work yourself. What else does he do for you, Nymphomaniac Nimmi? Whore through and through!"

"Are you quite done?" she asked when he paused for breath. She wiped his spittle from her face coolly though she was quaking inside.

"Done? Oh no! I'm just getting started. I'm actually being nice because women like you deserve public shaming, no? But I won't take this further, see, because I know you can't help it. You have slut blood. Your mother had it, and your grandmother before her. You've all fucked anything that moves." Nimmi was aghast. How had she ever cared for this vile man? She tried to get up but he slapped her down, eliciting another gasp from her.

"So, was it good with this *banchod*? Did he take you from behind like the bitch you are? Did you beg for more?"

Something popped in Nimmi's head. Screaming as she repeatedly struck his chest, she succeeded in shoving him off her and onto the floor. She stood over him then, massive stomach riding high. "I'm the whore? Really? Who goes wherever he can smell money? Who kisses ass for the most minor leg-up? Who betrayed his patients in Kolkata when he rammed the wrong medicine down their throats for pharmaceutical kickbacks? A patient died, didn't he? How many others did?" She made her way across the room as she remembered. "It was a rumour nobody would substantiate for me. And we were expecting a baby. So, I agreed to join you here." At the back door, she turned to say, "I'm done with this." Then she walked into the night.

In the garden what little cool she had left dissolved into tears. The baby lurched, as if distraught too. This heightened Nimmi's anxiety. Everything was much more complicated with a baby on the way, beloved though it was. She found she couldn't think straight but her feet knew what they were doing as it guided her down her usual path. To the wall. It was pitch-dark but having walked to it every day for the last month or more, she had no trouble finding her way. The path was springy with the flowers that persisted in falling at her feet daily. She heard the swing creaking in its glade. Then she smelt the cherry blossoms, and knew she was at the last stand of flowering trees before the garden sloped to the wall. Navigating in the night had been made easier by the work Edric put in a couple of weeks ago. It was almost as if he had cleared her way knowingly.

Edric. And the kids. There would be sanctuary there, and time to think. But where was 'there'? Her feet knew though. They were mounting the wall. It was low on her side. And she was standing atop before long. Teetering was closer to the truth, the weight of her stomach tipping her over the edge. Over that edge, a long way down, were her friends. She had seen their green and inviting forest dwelling. She craved the comfort it represented but the heft of her stomach now made her stop and question herself. Were Edric and the children really down there? Or anywhere at all outside her head? Was she about to send herself and her baby hurtling down a sheer drop to bone-smashingly hard ground or to a safe haven? The questions came at her with the force of the bitterly cold winds she'd experienced in her first weeks in Nottingham. Like the latter they slapped her into wakefulness.

She took a step back. Then two. "No," she said aloud, "another way will present itself. Tomorrow." She was about to step down when two hands gripped her ankles firmly. Two strong, work-roughened hands pulled her off the wall.

Into the other side.

# A Time to Keep
*Alan Sillitoe*

Martin drew the cloth from the kitchen table. An old tea-stain made a map of Greenland when held up to the light. He folded it into an oblong and laid it on the dresser.

After the anxiety of getting his brother and sister to bed he lifted his books from the cupboard and spread them over the bare wood, where they would stay till the heart-catching click of the gate latch signalled his parents' return.

He was staying in to see that the fire did not go out, and to keep the light on. He was staying up because he was older. When that unmistakable click of the gate latch sounded he would set a kettle on the gas to make coffee. Funny how thirsty they still were after being in the boozer all night. His two-hour dominion over the house would be finished, but as consolation he could give in to the relief of knowing that they had not after all been hit by a bus and killed.

Most of the books had been stolen. None had been read from end to end. When opened they reeked of damp from bookshop shelves. Or they stank from years of storage among plant pots and parlour soot.

He put a French grammar on to *Peveril of the Peak*, and a Bible in Polish on top of that. The clock could be heard now that they were out and he had extinguished the television. He sang a tune to its ticking under his breath, then went back to his books. He would start work next year, and didn't know whether he wanted to or not. Things could go on like this for ever as far as he was concerned. You got booted out of school, though, at fifteen, and that was that.

The certainty that one day he would be pushed into a job had hovered around him since he first realized as a child that his father went out every morning in order to earn money with which to feed them, pay the rent, get clothes, and keep a roof over their heads. His mother used these phrases, and they stabbed into him like fire. At that time work had nothing to do with him, but it soon would have. It was a place of pay and violence which his father detested, to judge by the look on his face when he came home every evening with his snapsack and teacan.

Under the dark space of the stairs he shovelled around for coal to bank up the dull fire — a pleasurable task, as long as the flames came back to life. A hole in the pan needed bigger lumps set over it so that cobbles and slack wouldn't spill on the mat between the coal-heap and grate. They'd rather have a few pints of beer than buy a dustpan.

He washed his hands in the scullery. He liked soap that was keen to the smell. Arranging his chair, he sat down again and lifted the cover of a beige leather-bound volume of French magazines. He read a sentence under the picture: a bridge over the River Seine near Rouen. In other books he was able to put Portuguese or Italian phrases into English. When a word appealed to his sight he manoeuvred through the alphabet of a dictionary to get at its meaning, though he never tried to learn a language properly. He handled books like a miser. In each one his name was written in capital letters, though there was no danger of them being stolen, because they were gold that could not be spent. The strange kind of hunger he felt in looking at them often fixed him into a hypnosis that stopped him using them properly.

If burglars came they would nick the television, not books. They were stacked according to size, then sorted in their various languages. Excitement led him to range them from high at both ends to small in the middle. He bracketed them between a tea-caddy and a box of his father's car tools so that none could escape. Then he spread them out again, like playing cards.

Summer was ending. It seemed as if it always was. He had a bike, but Friday night was too much of a treat to go out. He also thought it a squander of precious daylight on his parents' part that they should have been in the pub for an hour before it got dark. And yet, as soon as the outside walls and chimney pots were no longer clear, he swung the curtains decisively together, pushing away what little of the day was left. Once it was going, he wanted to be shut of it. He switched on glowing light that made the living room a secret cave no one could get into.

His parents were used to his daft adoration of books, but for anyone beyond the family to witness his vital playthings would make him blush with shame. Aunts, cousins and uncles would mock him, but what else could you expect? If it hadn't been that, they'd have teased him for something else. They had never actually seen his books, though they had been laughingly told about them by his parents. Books and the people he knew didn't belong together, and that was a fact, but he knew it was impossible to live without either.

He wondered what other eyes had slid across these pages. Their faces could be frightening, or happy. They had come in out of the rain after doing a murder. Or they closed a book and put it down so as to go out and do a good deed. How did you know? You never did. You had to make it all up and scare yourself daft.

In any case, how had they felt about what they were reading? What houses had they lived in, and what sort of schools had they gone to? Did they like their furniture? Did they hate their children? He would rather have been any one of those people than himself. Maybe nobody had read the books. They got them as presents, or bought them and forgot to read them. The thought made him feel desolate, though not for long. Books always took his mind off the world around. He lifted the picture-album of France, and pondered on every voyage the book had made. It had been to Chile and China, and all the other places he could think of, between leaving the printers' and reaching his table in Radford.

A clatter of footsteps at the yard-end and the boisterous notes of a voice he did not at first recognize dragged him clear. Print had hooks, but they were made of rubber. Before the warning click of the gate latch his dozen volumes were scooped off the table and stacked on the floor behind the far side of the dresser.

By the time the door opened the gas was lit and a full kettle set on it. He put sugar, milk and a bottle of coffee on the table, then sat looking through a car magazine as if he hadn't moved all evening. His cousin Raymond was first in the room. No stranger, after all. His mother and father breathed a strong smell of ale.

"He's the quickest lad I know at getting that kettle on the burning feathers!" his father said. "A real marvel at it. I drove like a demon back from the Crown for my cup o' coffee."

"And you nearly hit that van coming out of Triumph Road," Raymond laughed.

Martin wondered whether he should take such praise as it was intended, or hate his father for imagining that he needed it, or despise him for thinking he could get round him in such a way. He was already taller than his father, and there were times when he couldn't believe it, and occasions when he didn't like it, though he knew he had to get used to it. So had his father, but he didn't seem bothered by such a thing. He decided to ignore the praise, though he *had* got the kettle on in record time.

"You brought him up right," Raymond hung his jacket on the back of the door. "He worn't drug up, like me." He bumped into his aunt. "Oops, duck, mind yer back, yer belly's in danger!"

Martin laughed, without knowing whether he wanted to or not. His father would put up with anything from Raymond, who had been to Approved School, Detention Centre and Borstal, though he was now an honest man of twenty-two, and able to charm anybody when he wanted. He did it so well that you were convinced he would never get caught stealing again. He could also use a bullying, jocular sort of self-confidence, having learned how to live rough, half-inch a thing or two, and die young if he must, without getting sent down every year for a Christmas box or birthday present. Another lesson well taken was that he must always look smart, talk clear and act quick, so that anyone who mattered would think he could be trusted. At Borstal he had done boxing, because it seemed that both God and the Governor were on the side of those who stored the deadliest punch. He had developed one as fast as he could, and wasn't afraid to use it whenever necessary. He was loyal to his family, helping them with money and goods to the best of his ability and hard work. He was often heard to say that he couldn't go back to his old ways, for his mother's sake.

Martin wanted to be like his cousin, though sensing that he might never be so made him look up to him even more. He was certainly glad he'd got the books out of sight before he came in.

Raymond, with his bread and cheese, and cup of coffee, was first to sit down. Martin moved across the room, leaving the fire to the grownups. The yellow flames blazed for them alone, and for their talk that came from the big world of boozers that he hadn't yet entered but was avid to. Raymond stretched out a leg, and expertly belched the words: "Pardon me!" — at which they all laughed.

He held his cup for more coffee. "I'll be off to Alfreton again in the morning. Help to build another mile o' that motorway. You know how it's done, don't you? I open my big gob wide. Somebody shovels tar and concrete in. Then I walk along shitting out motorway and coughing up signposts!"

"It'll soon be as far as Leeds, wain't it?" his father said quickly, trying to head off such remarks, which he found a bit too loud-mouthed.

Raymond detected the manoeuvre, and to save face, turned censorious: "It would be, Joe, if everybody got cracking at their job. But they're too busy looting to get much done. The fields for miles on either side are laid waste by plundering navvies. Some of 'em sit around smoking and talking, and waiting for a turnip to show itself above the soil. As soon as it does, up it comes! They go straight into their snapsacks."

He was a joker. They weren't sure whether it was true or not. No gaffer could afford to let you get away with not working full-tilt. But he *had* brought vegetables home. Ripping up a basketful was the work of a few minutes in the dusk: "A bloke the other day came to wok in his minivan," Raymond told them, "and drove it a little way into the wood. He kept the engine running so's we wouldn't hear his chain-saw, but when I went in for a piss I saw the bleeder stacking logs in the back. A nice young pine tree had gone, and he covered the stump up wi' leaves. Nowt's safe. It's bleddy marvellous. He's going to get caught one day, doing it in the firm's time!"

Martin seemed born to listen. Maybe it went with collecting books. If he read them properly he'd perhaps start talking a bit more, and it might be easier then to know what other people were thinking.

"He don't say much," Raymond observed, "our Martin don't, does he?"

But he did at school. Among his pals he was as bright as an Amazon parrot. If he tackled a book properly, on the other hand, he might talk even less. It was hard to say until he did. Cut anybody's finger off who got too fresh. The teacher once stopped him bashing up another boy, and said if he caught him at it again he'd pull his arm off. He couldn't really be like Raymond, who'd once got chucked out of school for hitting a teacher right between the eyes.

"He'll be at work next year," his mother nodded at Martin. "It's looney to keep 'em till they're fifteen, big kids like him. Give him summat to do. *And* bring us some money in."

"The bloody road tax is twenty-five quid now," his father said bitterly, and Martin felt as if he were being blamed for it.

"I didn't have one for six months last year," Raymond boasted. "I stuck an old Guinness label on the windscreen. Nobody twigged it."

Martin knew it wasn't true.

"You never did!" his father said, who believed it. "I wish I'd had such an idea."

"No, I tell a lie. It was only on for a fortnight. Then I got the wind up, and bought a real 'un." He turned his grey eyes on to Martin, as if embarrassed by somebody who didn't continually give themselves away in speech. "I'll get our Martin a job wi' me on the motorway, though," he said. "That'll settle his hash. He'll come home every night absolutely knackered."

I expect I might, Martin thought. "What would I do?"

"You'd have to get up early, for a start."

That wouldn't bother him. Lots of people did. "What time's that?"

"Six."

"He's dead to the wide at six. It's all I can do to get him out of bed by eight o'clock."

"I'm not, our mam."

Raymond looked at the fire, as if he would have spat at the bars if it had been in his own home. "I pass here in my car at half past. I'll pick you up tomorrow, if you like."

"Will yer be fit for it?" his father wanted to know.

Martin, taking more coffee and another slice of bread, didn't think he'd heard right. He often looked at the opening of a book, and when he understood every word, couldn't believe he'd read it properly, and then went back to make sure. "Tomorrow?"

"Well, I din't say owt about yesterday, did I?"

If Raymond said something, he meant it. He often said that you must regret nothing, and that you should always keep promises. It helped his reputation of being a man who showed up in a crowd. So he promised something in a loud voice now and again in order to keep himself up to scratch. "I'll stop my owd banger outside the Co-op. If you're there I'll take you. If you ain't, I'll just push on."

"I'll be waiting." Martin felt like one of those sailors in the olden days who, about to set off west, wasn't sure he would ever get back again.

The sky was clear and cold. He saw it over the housetops, and above the façade of the bingo hall that he first went into as a cinema one Saturday afternoon nearly ten years ago.

The wet road looked as clean as if a light shone on it. He buttoned the jacket over his shirt. You never wore a top coat to work unless you were one of the older men. It was too early for traffic, making the road look different to when it was pounded by buses and lorries during the day. His mother had disturbed him from a hundred feet under the sand below the deepest part of the ocean when she had tried to wake him. She had to grab the clothes off him in the end.

Sandwiches bulged in his pocket. He enjoyed waiting, but his hands were cold. "Never put your hands in your pockets when you're on the job," Raymond had said. "A lot of 'em do, but it don't look good." He couldn't do it while waiting to go there, either. He wished he were setting off to work properly, and that he didn't have another year to do before he got real wages. There wasn't much point in starting work today, and then next year as well.

A postman went by on a bike. "Morning, kid."

"Morning."

Raymond's car had rust along the bottom of the door as it swung open towards him. "Get in."

He sounded disappointed that Martin had been able to meet him. The car sailed up Wollaton Road like an aeroplane, spun around the traffic island by the Crown, and went along Western Boulevard. "Tired?"

"It's a treat, being up early."

"Bring owt t'eat?"

"Yeh. Mam forgot some tea, though."

"I've got a mashing." He played the car with hands and feet as if on a big picture-house organ. "Sugar, tea, and tinned milk — solid like a cannon ball. Enough for a battalion. Trust our mam. She's old-fashioned, but she's a marvel all the same. You can stand a garden fork in *her* strong tea."

Beyond the town there was a cloud like a big white dog. Martin yawned, and expected it to do the same.

"We like to start as soon as daylight hits," Raymond went on. "That's where the money is, in overtime. You don't mind getting out o' yer warm bed when you can mek a bit of money. I'd wok all hours God sends, for money.

Watch the tax, though. Bastards will skin you dry, and fry you rotten. Dangerous work, as well. Nearly got scooped up by a mechanical digger the other day. But it's money that I like to be getting into my pocket, fartin' Martin! As soon as I know there's money to be earned I'd dig that soil up with my fingernails. They don't need to tell me when to start sweating!"

Martin had a question. "What do you do with it?"

"Wi' what?"

"The money you get."

"Ah! Booze a bit — that's me. Treat everybody — now and again. Save a lot, though. Gonna buy a house when I've got the deposit. Me and mam'll live in it. Not the other spongers, though. They wain't get a look in."

His brothers and sisters had reputations as scroungers. Serve 'em right if Raymond dealt with them as they deserved.

The narrow lane was so rutted he thought they'd get stuck, the car swaying from side to side, sharp privet branches scraping the window. The wheels skidded on the mud in a couple of places, but it didn't bother Raymond. He steered as if in a rally car, then grumbled: "Fuckers should have cut that hedge down," — seeing in his mirror another car grinding too closely behind.

As they topped the rise tears of muddy water lashed against the windscreen. When the wipers flushed over it Martin saw the vast clayey cutting between green banks. It was a man-made valley occupied by lorries, cranes, mechanical diggers. Those already moving seemed to be the ones that owned it. He was surprised at how few men there were, having expected to see them swarming all over the place.

Raymond drove parallel to the valley, and parked his car by a cluster of huts. He got out, and farted, then stretched his arms and legs. "See that trailer?"

"Yes."

"Well, I'm going to book myself in."

The nearest wooden hut, full of tools, smelt as if it were made of still-growing trees. He expected to tread on leaves as he went in to have a look, but there was a crunch of gravel under his boots. His eyes were sore from little sleep. He yawned while trying to stretch his arms without being seen.

The sound of engines moaned and jerked from the canyon. They formed a chorus. There was never silence. Raw earth was being cleared. Soon it would be covered, and packed, and solidified, and paved to take traffic and huge lorries between London and Leeds. The men who did it knew what their work was for. They could see it as plain as a streak of paint across a piece of new wood. But it must go so slowly that a month was like a day.

Raymond came back wearing a helmet and a livid pink jacket. "Don't stand idle," he called sharply, so that Martin didn't know whether he was joking or not. "Let's get on that motor."

The dumper truck swayed as it went down the track hewn in the incline. The narrow ledge frightened him, for the dumper might tumble any minute and take both of them to the bottom. Raymond fought with the wheel and gears, laughed and swore as he swung it zig-zag along.

"This fucking thing — it's like a dog: I tamed it a long while ago, so you've no need to worry." The machine went more quickly. "If we don't get down in one piece, though, I'll get the push. That's the sort of world we're living in, Martin. Owt happens to this dumper, and I get my cards. Don't matter about us, if we get killed. We'll get compo, but what good does that do yer?"

He drove the petrol-smelling truck under the digger to take its load, then lumbered it back up the escarpment in such a way that Martin didn't think he'd tamed it at all. Tipping it from above helped to heighten the embankment. "The bleeding gaffer wanted to know what you was doing here, so I told him you was the new mash-lad from Cresswell. He's got so much on his plate though, that gaffer, that he don't know whether he's coming or going. Looked a bit gone-out at me, burree din't say owt."

After two trips Martin decided to stay on top. He could watch the beetling dumpers doing their work from a distance, which was better than being down among them. He remembered a word from school that would describe the long deep scar: geology, geological. The layers of gravel and grit and clay were being sliced like a cake so that the motorway could be pushed through into Yorkshire.

In a while he sat down. It was a struggle to keep the eyes open when you weren't thinking about anything. The wind died and the sun came out. He was dozing in its warm beams, then dreaming, but he never cut off from the distant punch and rumble of machinery, and the occasional shouting that broke through as if finding him at the end of a long search.

Diesel smoke wafted across. He opened his eyes so as not to lose contact with the sort of work he hoped to be getting paid for next year. Raymond nudged him awake: "You poor bogger! A bit too early in the morning, was it?"

"No, it worn't," he snapped.

"You know why, though, don't you?" He had a can of hot tea, and offered him the lid as a cup. "Take this. I'll get some scoff."

"Why?" The sweet strong tea went straight to the waking-up box behind his eyes.

"You stayed up too late. Can't go to work early if you don't get to your wanking pit on time. Not unless you're over eighteen, anyway. You'll 'ave to stop reading all them books. Send you blind."

He'd heard that before — often. "I'm not tired."

Raymond rolled a neat cigarette. "What about some snout, then?"

"No, thanks."

He laughed. Smoke drifted from his open mouth. "That's right. Keep off the fags. Don't booze, either, or go with women. Stick to your books as long as you can. And you know why? I'll tell yer: because fags pack your lungs in, booze softens your brain, and women give you the clap."

With that, he went back to work.

Martin didn't know what to make of such advice, so it didn't seem important. He wished he had one of the books he'd stacked and shifted about on the table last night, even if it was only the Bible in Polish, or the Italian dictionary. When dumper trucks again moved into the canyon, and the first one came back loaded, they didn't interest him any more, though he thought they might if he sat at the wheel of one like Raymond.

An hour later he was so bored that he felt hungry, so finished off his last cheese sandwich. Sitting high up and set apart gave him a picture-view. Nothing happened, and he was bored, yet everything moved so slowly that he wouldn't forget it as long as he lived.

Raymond's truck was easy to recognize. He saw clearly across the whole distance, and watched him go with his load up the far slope of the motorway. A wind blew from the streets of a town on the skyline, as if someone on the church top in the middle were wafting it over. With his vivid sight he saw Raymond's truck go behind a long low spoil bank, the helmet moving slowly. Then his body reappeared, and finally the truck again.

It was manoeuvred into a clearing for about the twentieth time, and guided close to the escarpment by another man. It waited a few seconds, as if to get breath, then it tipped its load. There was no pause before setting off quickly towards the excavation for another.

He stared more closely, imagining he was Raymond sitting on the truck and working the levers, confidently steering after four years' experience, smelling old oil and new soil and wondering how much he would coin that day. He wouldn't mind working here, even if he did have to start by seeing to the men's tea and running errands from one hut to another. A mash-lad was better than a school-kid.

The truck reversed towards the precipice at a normal and careful speed. At dusk they'd drive back to Nottingham. Maybe Raymond would call at home for a bite to eat before going to where he lived in the Meadows — though it wasn't likely because he never went visiting in his working clothes.

He could almost hear the engines speeding up. "I'll get this one over with," Raymond might be saying, "then I'll pack it in and piss off out of it. Done enough graft for one day." He sensed the words going through his brain. He said them aloud, as if to save his cousin the thought or energy.

He couldn't say who was tired most: him, Raymond, or the man whom Raymond's dumper truck knocked flying over the almost sheer slope. The man had sauntered out of the way as usual but then, for a reason which was hard to make out (though he was sure there must have been one, since there always was a reason — for everything), he leapt back against the truck as if to dive underneath.

It wasn't easy to decide the exact point of impact. The man's spade turned in the air, and Martin swore he heard the clatter as its metal head caught the side of the truck.

The body rolled down the steep bank and smashed into a mechanical digger. He watched Raymond jump from his seat. Other men lined the top of the spoil heap. Two or three, Raymond clearly among them, started to scramble down.

The whole heart-side of Martin's body was dulled with pain. It lasted a few seconds, then left him feeling cold, wind-blown and gritty at the eyes, which now seemed to lose their vision. The sound of an ambulance came from far away as he walked towards the huts. His legs and arms shivered as if from cold. He gripped himself till it stopped. The flashing blue lights of a police car bobbed along the hedge-top.

He noticed how pale Raymond was when he got into the car an hour after his usual knocking-off time. He smoked a cigarette, something he said he never did when driving. "That pig-copper told me I'd killed 'im on purpose," he shouted above the engine as it roared and sent the car skidding along the muddy lane. "They said I must have been larking about."

"I didn't see yer, and I was watching."

"A few others was as well, so I'm all right for witnesses. But can you believe it? Killed 'im on purpose! One of the blokes I'd known for weeks! Can you imagine him asking a thing like that? Must be rotten to the bloody core. He just jumped in front of my truck."

Martin felt as if he was asking the only question in his life that needed a proper answer:

"Why did he do it?"

After half a minute's silence, which seemed so long that Martin thought his cousin would never speak again, unless to tell him to mind his own business, Raymond said: "You won't guess. Nobody on this earth would. I'll tell yer, though. He dropped his packet o' fags in front of my truck, and because he thought the wheels would crush 'em, he jumped to pick 'em up. The daft bastard didn't want to lose his fags. Would you believe it? Didn't *think*! Blokes who don't think deserve all they get. I'd have given him half of my own fags though, if only he'd left 'em alone." He smiled bleakly at his untested generosity. "Can't understand him doing a thing like that. I thought I knew him, but bogger me if I did. You don't know anybody, *ever* Martin. So never think you do."

"He's dead now, though."

"The daft bleeder."

Martin said he was sorry it happened. He hated feeling the tears at his eyes as sharp as glass. "Who was he?"

"An old chap, about forty-odd. Happy old chokker. He was allus singing, he was. You could tell from his mouth, but nobody ever heard him because of the engines kicking up such a noise. He didn't sing when he thought we could hear him. Funny bloke altogether. All my life I've been careful, though, that's the best on it. I never wanted that to happen. I'm not a murderer, it don't matter what that copper tried to say. 'I'm not a murderer, your honour! Honest, I'm not!' That's what I'll shout out in court when the case comes up."

Back in the lighted streets, Martin said nothing. He had nothing to say, because everything had been *done*. His cousin drove with one hand, and held his wrist tight when he reached across with the other. "I'm glad you came to work with me today, any road up, our Martin. I wouldn't have liked to drive home on my own after that little lot. I'll tek you right to your door. Don't say owt to your mam and dad, though, will yer?"

"Why?"

"Let me tell 'em, tomorrer." He was on the edge of crying. Martin never thought he'd feel sorry for Raymond, but he did now. He felt more equal than he'd ever done — and even more than that. There wasn't much to look up to. The big mauler was crushing his wrist. "Aren't you going to the boozer with 'em tonight?"

He drew his hand off, to change gear before stopping at the White Horse traffic lights. "I think I'll get off home. Mam might go out and get me a bottle of ale from the beer-off." He winked. "If I ask her nice." Nothing could keep him down for long.

Martin wasn't as tired as he had been by the motorway. When his parents drove to the boozer he got his books out of the dresser, instead of going to the last house at the pictures as was usual on Saturday night.

The clear clean print was a marvel to his eyes. He started to read the first page, then became so drawn into the book that he didn't even hear the click of the gate latch when it sounded three hours later.

# The Contributors

**John Harvey** came originally to Nottingham as a teacher, from there became a student and then, finally, a writer. Poet, dramatist and one-time small press publisher, he is best known as a writer of crime fiction, in particular for his twelve-volume Nottingham-based series of police procedurals featuring Charlie Resnick, the last of which, *Darkness, Darkness*, he is currently turning into a stage play for Nottingham Playhouse and New Perspectives Theatre Company. In 2007, he was awarded the Crime Writers' Association Cartier Diamond Dagger for Sustained Excellence in Crime Writing, and in 2009 he was awarded an honorary degree, Doctor of Letters, by the University of Nottingham.

**Megan Taylor's** first novel, *How We Were Lost*, a dark coming-of-age story, was published by Flame Books in 2007 after placing second in the 2006 Yeovil Prize. She wrote her second, *The Dawning,* while studying for an MA in Creative Writing at Manchester Metropolitan University. *The Dawning,* a domestic thriller set over the course of a single night, was published by Weathervane Press in 2010. Megan's third novel, *The Lives of Ghosts* (Weathervane, 2012), plays with ideas of inheritance and motherhood, and the haunting power of memories that refuse to be suppressed. Her first short story collection, *The Woman Under the Ground*, illustrated by Nikki Pinder, was released in 2014, again by Weathervane. Megan lives in Nottingham with her two children.

For too long **Brick** has been a political cartoonist and comics creator and, as **John Stuart Clark**, author of adventure travel articles and books. With five cartoon and two prose books and a couple of breakdowns to his name, he is also a volunteer forest ranger and (somehow) Honorary Associate Professor at the University of Nottingham's School of English. His present diversion is a graphic investigation into *The Curious Case of Leonardo's Bicycle*, due to be published this year. He has been based in Nottingham since the late 1960s.

**Paula Rawsthorne** is an award-winning Young Adult writer. Paula came to university in Nottingham over twenty years ago and never left. She was a winner of The Society of Children's Book Writers' and Illustrators, Undiscovered Voices 2010. Her novels, *The Truth About Celia Frost* and *Blood Tracks,* are published by Usborne. *Celia Frost* was shortlisted for eleven literary awards, winning The Leeds Book Award (2012), Sefton Super Reads Award (2012), and the Nottingham Brilliant Book Award (2013). Her second novel, *Blood Tracks*, has been shortlisted for several literary awards, winning The Rib Valley Book Award 2014. Her short stories for adults have been published by Route. Her comic story, *The Sermon on the Mount*, won a national BBC competition and was read by Bill Nighy on BBC Radio 4. She's invited to do author visits in secondary schools throughout the country and is a writer-in-residence for the literacy charity *First Story*. She's a member of Nottingham Writers' Studio and SCBWI-BI.

**Alison Moore** was born in Manchester in 1971. Her short fiction has been included in *Best British Short Stories* and *Best British Horror* anthologies and broadcast on BBC Radio 4 Extra. The title story of her debut collection *The Pre-War House and Other Stories* won a *New Writer* novella prize. Her first novel, *The Lighthouse*, was shortlisted for the Man Booker Prize 2012 and the

National Book Awards 2012 (New Writer of the Year), and won the McKitterick Prize 2013. Her second novel, *He Wants*, was published in 2014. She lives in a village on the Leicestershire-Nottinghamshire border, is an honorary lecturer at Nottingham University and a member of Nottingham Writers' Studio.

**Shreya Sen Handley** is a Calcutta-born, Nottingham-based mother of two. She is a former television journalist and producer for channels including CNBC and MTV, who now writes and illustrates for the British and Indian media. A columnist for the *National Geographic, Times of India* and *Nottingham Post*, she has also written for *The Guardian,* CNN India and *The Hindu*, amongst other sites and publications. A children's book she illustrated for Hachette was published in 2014 and her memoir, for Harper Collins, on which she is currently working, is slated for the summer of 2016.

**Alan Sillitoe** is best known for his first novel and subsequent collection of short stories, *Saturday Night and Sunday Morning* and *The Loneliness of the Long Distance Runner*. He also wrote the screenplay of the films based on *Saturday Night* and the title story of *Loneliness*. Subsequently he wrote several collections of poetry, short stories, children's books, travel writing and many further novels, about half of which were based in his native Nottingham (where a tram is named after him!). In autumn of 2015 there will be a festschrift published in his honour in Nottingham. Alan Sillitoe died in 2010.